Being Kate

Rita Trotman is the author of:

Take Three Boys - a memoir set in Romania

The Way It Is - a novel set in a boys' boarding school

Small Words – a collection of short stories

Nothing Like A Dame – a memoir set in Eton College

Tiger Tails – an illustrated children's book

Wedding Fever - a three act play

The Elves and the Shoemaker - a pantomime

Cinderella -a pantomime

Being Kate

by

Rita Trotman

First published in 2024

Copyright Rita Trotman

All characters in this book are fictitious and any resemblance to real persons is purely coincidental.

All rights reserved.

No part of this publication may be reproduced, stored in a retrieval system, or transmitted in any form without the permission of the author in writing.

ISBN: 9798326892119

Cover photography Stepan Kulyk

With thanks to:

Eric Trotman

Rob Courtice

June Cohen

For Monica

Being Kate

Prologue

Kate 1970

I decided to shoot myself with my father's gun a month before my eleventh birthday. The process for my demise was carefully planned as failure was not an option.

Step one - time Bitch-Mother's movements when she shuts the hens up for the night, and step two - choose a location in which to execute the deed. I was an avid reader and a lonely child, well used to playing solitary games.

For weeks I shadowed Bitch-Mother's trips to the henhouse each evening and snooped on her from my den in the beech tree. I watched as she gathered eggs, filled the hen's water bowls and secured the birds for the night. She always checked the wire fence to ensure marauding foxes couldn't eat her clucky babies. I noted all movements and charted them in a spiral-bound notebook with a biro found in my homework satchel.

My den in the beech tree was the hiding place for my treasures so I hid the notebook and pen in one of Bitch-Mother's screw top jars and placed them alongside my collection of coloured glass and the bottle of perfume I'd made with petals from the summer roses. Notes to self - *it takes Bitch-Mother ten minutes to shut the chickens in for the night, longer if the cockerel refuses to vacate the holly tree.*

I was confident that ten minutes would be sufficient time to fire a gun. Other crucial information included - *Father attends his meeting on Wednesday nights and leaves the house at six fifteen precisely.*

The calculated time slot occurred at six nineteen on a Wednesday in October. I had already placed a note under my pillow to inform the world of the terrible burden life had inflicted on one so young and asked for my doll to be buried with me.

I chose the dining room to bear witness to my demise. I liked the landscape painting above the fireplace and imagined I'd gaze upon it as I passed.

Having watched Bitch-Mother slide into her welly boots that evening and leave by the back door, I carefully lifted the shotgun from the hall cupboard. My heart raced as I caressed its polished rosewood insets and inhaled a pungent essence of oily rag.

I carried the gun with care and settled myself against the wall where I stared at the painting, admired the grazing cows and a babbling brook, and imagined heaven would be similar. But as I dragged the shotgun into my lap, an immense problem unfolded.

It became clear that the logistics of the mission were outside the capabilities of one so young. To my dismay I found both the size, weight and unfamiliarity of the gun were detrimental to the plan, and I was heartily fed-up. I had hoped a dead girl in a pink and white gingham dress and ankle socks would have upset even Bitch-Mother, particularly if I bled-out on the parquet floor and my brains ruined her floral wallpaper. I visualised the spoilt-brat Yorkshire terrier paddling through my blood, its paws creating a mosaic on the floor. I confess I had an unhealthy imagination for one so young.

I couldn't have known of course, at such a tender age, that there would be no cartridge in the gun or of the physical impossibility of the whole affair. It was a naive, flawed plan, mostly because short arms and a long shotgun shredded all hope of an outcome.

I could hardly believe there was a snag. But no matter how hard I tried to support the weight of the gun I couldn't get the barrel near any part of my body. I took a deep breath and tried to reconfigure the methodology.

I sat so long in contemplation, fighting tears of frustration and disbelief, that Bitch-Mother returned from the chickens and found me. I have no recollection of what she said or what lie I invented; I do, however, remember the beating I received for touching my father's gun.

I vowed to get the better of Bitch-Mother one day. I imagined I would drag her over the grassy bank and roll her in chicken shit until she screamed for mercy. 'Stop it, Katherine. Stop it,' she'd yell. But I would keep on beating her with the stick she'd used on me.

As it turned out, I never had the satisfaction of living out that childhood fantasy. Instead, I take pleasure in stomping on Bitch-Mother's grave. I accept I'm a fully grown adult who should know better, but I don't.

Chapter 1

Jono Symonds rang Kate's doorbell thirteen months, four days and six hours after the death of her husband, Chris. It was almost Spring and frost shone like sugar-crystals on the holly tree. A post-Christmas malaise had settled among the flowerbeds and newly sprung tulips were nipped by the frost. Despite the desolation of winter hanging around the garden, Jono Symonds noted the detached, brick-built house was well cared for. A scarlet, soft-top lurked under the car port like a blob of tabasco sauce.

The doorbell unsettled Kate. She peered through the bedroom window although her line of sight revealed nothing more than a smudge of black. She pulled on a warm jumper and smoothed her hair, trying to decide if the caller could be ignored. *For pity's sake. You're scared of your own shadow. You're becoming a recluse. You only need a couple of cats to complete the look. Chris would be ashamed of you.*

She dabbed her favourite russet lipstick to her mouth and descended the stairs two at a time. *Damn. I'm late.* Her children were due to spill into the school playground in less than thirty minutes, and there were still traffic lights on Tobacconist Road. Even if she went the long way around, up Kirby Hill and behind the pharmacy, she was still leaving it tight.

The doorbell echoed a second attempt to gain her attention. Kate picked up Tom's Action Man from the floor and placed it on the Habitat sofa while noticing the plug-in room fragrance was empty.

With undisguised resignation she answered the door to a leather-clad stranger. The biting wind streamed past her into the warm house. Kate looked at him and fought resentment when he offered his wide smile. *What's so great about your life? No one dead then?* A motorbike helmet lingered in one hand and a paperback-sized parcel in the other. There was a hot, black BMW motorbike parked beside him, tick ticking as the engine cooled. She looked from him to the parcel and back to his face.

'Yes?'

'This is a personal delivery for Mrs. Katherine Roseland,' he told her. His smile set off a row of perfectly white teeth. 'Is that you?'

'Yes, but I'm not expecting anything.' *That was almost rude.* Kate squeezed the door open a fraction in recompense and felt the chilly air invade her chunky, hand-knitted jumper 'Are you sure?'

'I'm sure. It's from GCHQ,' he told her.

Blood leached from Kate's face and she leaned against the door to support her knees. *It's still not over. When will it be over?* She hugged herself as the icy wind sucked warmth from her body. He asked if she was OK. *Do I look as if I'm fucking OK?*

'Can I bring it in? The parcel? Perhaps you need to sit down.'

Kate waved a hand and he walked in, closing the door behind him. *Be my guest.*

'Can I get you a glass of water?' Concern showed on his face. 'I'm Jonathan Symonds by the way. But known as Jono.' He made a gallant half-bow by way of introduction. His classic English skin-tone was pleasing on the eye - to any eye that cared to notice.

He marched through the house and found the kitchen and there they perched on the chrome stools next to the breakfast-bar. The package sat on the green Formica work-surface while her eyes glanced from the parcel to his face.

Something that size can hardly be significant. Can it?

'I'll need your autograph,' he told her.

Her hand shook as she scrawled her signature on Jono's delivery note which he dragged from the depth of his biker-jacket pocket. '

'Why you? Why did GCHQ send it with you?' *Rude again. Try harder. It isn't his fault your life is a mess.*

Jono appeared not to notice. He told her about his courier company in Cheltenham. 'I send vans and motorbikes all over Europe, always with precious cargo and a lot of my work is with GCHQ.' He levelled his questioning eyes at her. 'Pretty much everything I handle for them is either urgent or confidential.'

'My husband worked for GCHQ,' she said. 'Before a careless lorry driver killed him on the by-pass.'

Jono looked at her and his eyes deepened with concern. Unknown to either of them, he'd brought the last personal items belonging to Chris that had lingered in his workplace. *It was probably found at the back of a drawer by someone who never even knew him.*

Chris's personal belongings had been returned by his secretary, soon after his death. His desk-photo of the family, a coffee mug painted by the kids for Father's Day, a three months' salary cheque and details of the work insurance policy. There had also been a couple of decent pens and his diary. When she'd flicked through the pages her stomach had cramped at the sight of Chris's distinctive scrawl. It was only a diary, and it would have been vetted before it came to her, but she knew she would never part with it.

Now, it seemed, something had been overlooked and was being delivered by a stranger who seemed hell-bent on being helpful. *He's a bit like a Labrador puppy.* Jono stayed while she opened the parcel and helped her slit the tape as she fumbled with the task.

'Thanks.'

The package contained a seven year old life insurance

policy, an old wallet, empty except for a baby photo of the children, and a note from his boss apologising that the items had been 'overlooked.' He hoped Kate was managing to get her life back on track.

Like hell I am.

Jono made them both a cup of tea, taking charge of her kitchen as if he belonged there.

'How do you like your tea, Katherine?'

'Kate. I'm Kate, and with milk, no sugar.'

'I don't answer to Jonathan. I've always been Jono since I was a kid. You too?'

'No. I was always Katherine as a child.

He manoeuvred his way around Kate's designer kitchen, finding the fridge, teabags, and sugar. 'I'm afraid I'm a two spoonful sort of guy,' he told her apologetically, placing the sugar bowl on the worktop.

'Don't let my children hear that. They've both got a sweet tooth which is hard to combat.'

Two mugs of steaming tea appeared before her. Kate looked at her watch and excused herself. *Shit. The kids.* 'Thanks, but I must make a quick phone call.' She rang her friend Susie from the sitting room and asked if she could pick up the children from school.

'No probs. I'm just leaving. See you in a bit.' She didn't ask why; she just stepped in, no questions asked. *That's the sign of a good friend.*

'This should perk you up,' Jono said, sliding the mug of tea towards her as an invitation for her to drink it. 'But shouldn't it be sweet tea for shock?'

'Yuk. Not for me.'

'Nice garden,' he said, looking through the kitchen window.

'Are you trying to be funny? The garden's a mess.'

'Every garden's a mess in February. Should be some spring flowers about soon, though.'

'If the frost doesn't get them.'

Kate sipped her tea without another word. Small talk with strangers didn't really interest her, although she conceded he had charm. Gradually the colour returned to her cheeks.

'I do my mum's garden. She's getting too old to manage now that Dad's gone,' Jono told her.

He doesn't look like a Mummy's boy. Perhaps he's the real deal; maybe he's one of those rare, genuine blokes. He seems kind and caring. Like Chris, only not dead.

Jono studied Kate. 'You can't beat a cup of builder's tea, can you?' He sipped his with concentration. 'Can you bear to tell me about losing your husband? I understand if it's too painful.'

'It is.' But before Kate knew it, she was telling him about the tragedy. It came gushing out like a burst water main. She told him of the loneliness and the total pointlessness of the accident. And Jono was an attentive listener. If only Kate had invested more caution, she'd never have laid herself bare to a stranger. But it seemed natural; it felt right. And they were still perched on the kitchen stools when Tom and Hannah arrived home, courtesy of her friend Susie.

'Can't stop 'cos Chloe's got a piano lesson.' Susie raised an eyebrow at the shiny motorbike in the garden, gave Kate a beaming smile and was gone as quickly as she'd arrived.

'Thank you so much Suz. See you tomorrow.'

'Who's he?' Hannah demanded in the kitchen.

'Don't be rude Hannah. This is Jono and he's just leaving.'

'Hello Hannah. How was school?'

'All adults ask that. It was boring as usual.' She tugged at her school tie and threw it on a stool.

'Hannah, where are your manners?'

'Can I have hot Ribena?' The small girl gave Jono a sidelong glance.

'What's the magic word?'

'Abracadabra...? Is that magic enough?'

'Not clever and so the answer's no,' Kate said with a disapproving frown. 'Stop showing off.'

'Aw...'

'Is that your bike outside?' Tom's acceptance of strangers was a worry for Kate. His little-boy eyes lit the kitchen.

'It is. Are you into bikes?'

'Yeees. Could I sit on it? Please.' He looked at his mother for approval of his manners.

'What's your name, young man? If it's alright with your Mum, you're welcome to sit on my bike.'

'I'm Tom. I'm nearly six.'

'I suppose you can.' Kate looked doubtful. 'But it'll have to be quick. It's freezing out there.'

'Why does he get what he wants, but I can't have hot Ribena?'

'Because he has better manners than you.' Kate shot her daughter another warning look.

'Aw....'

'Aw nothing. Are you coming outside or not?'

'spose so.'

Kate wrapped the children in their coats which they'd abandoned on the hall floor, grabbed her peacoat and went outside. She remembered her camera and slipped back inside to grab it.

'And don't get any ideas about having a motorbike when you're older,' she told her son.

'It's awesome Mum. Really cool.' His tussled head which had Chris's double crown, bobbed with excitement.

'Who'd want to ride on *that*?' Hannah eyed the monstrosity with contempt.

Kate caught Jono's eye. 'It's because it isn't pink. She doesn't acknowledge any other colour these days.'

'Who'd want a pink one? Only a girl,' said Tom, making faces at his sister.

'Who'd want one any colour?' Hannah poked her tongue out at her brother.

Jono laughed and lifted Tom onto the monster bike. He looked so tiny that Kate gulped. *Why can't he have a Daddy to watch him grow up?* The small boy wanted to know what every dial was and how old Jono had been when he had his first motorbike.

'You're a real enthusiast, aren't you?' Jono ruffled Tom's tawny hair while Kate took a couple of photos.

'That's it, Tom. Jono has things to do, I'm sure.'

'Thanks,' Tom said as Kate prised him from the bike. His eyes were alight for the first time since he'd lost his father. 'Will you come and see the photos when Mum gets them printed?'

'Maybe,' said Jono, glancing at Kate.

'I'm starving Mum.' Tom headed inside.

'You don't know the difference between peckish and starving,' Kate called after him as she heard him thump up the stairs to shed his uniform. 'Starving happens in Africa. Remember?'

But she was shouting to the wind and Jono's eyes crinkled at the corners.

'There are biscuits and orange juice in the kitchen,' Kate told Hannah.

'Why not Ribena? You never let me have Ribena.' She didn't move and eyed the stranger with suspicion. 'Did you know my Daddy?' She sounded older than her years. 'He died you know.'

'No,' said Jono bending down to her eye level. 'I didn't know him, but Mummy told me about your Daddy and I'm so sorry.'

'Mummy says I have to say thank you when people say that to me. But I don't mean it. How can I say thank you that my Daddy is dead?'

'I'll bet it's hard, but you look very grown up to me.'

'Go and slip out of your uniform Humpy and see what Tom is up to.'

'Humpy?' Jono lifted an eyebrow at Kate. 'Humpy?'

'I know. It's probably time to let baby nicknames go but she was such a bolshie toddler, it's kind of stuck.' She paused. 'It was Chris who nicknamed her.'

'Daddy always called me Humpy but I'm getting a bit old for it now. Don't you think?'

'I think it's for you to decide. You'll know when you're ready to give it up,' Jono told her.

Hannah stared at Jono with questions in her eyes. She'd let her blonde hair escape from the ponytail Kate had taken so much care over that morning and something she'd had for school dinner sat on her white blouse.

'I'll bet you're eight,' said Jono.

'I'm seven and three quarters,' she told him, 'I know I look older.'

'You certainly do.'

'Go and change into your jeans, Darling. It's freezing out here.'

Hannah and Jono both stood sentry next to Kate; both were reluctant to leave her side.

Jono said, 'I'd better go and leave you in the capable hands of your children. Are you sure you're OK Kate?'

'Much better, thanks. Sorry if I appeared a bit wimpy.'

'You're anything but that. Don't be so hard on yourself. Let me know if I can do anything for you. Anything at all.' He picked up his helmet and gloves and slipped his business card into the pocket of her coat. *Sexy or what?*

'Thanks for bringing…' she glanced at Hannah, 'those things.'

'What things?' Hannah asked.

'Just something from a shop in Cheltenham,' Jono told Hannah. 'And it was my pleasure,' he told her mother, who looked into his eyes and couldn't look away.

Chapter 2

Kate

The news of my darling Chris's death arrived courtesy of two police officers who'd knocked with all the confidence of God Botherers. It was long before I had set eyes on Jono Symonds and, most importantly, it was a time when my life was nearly perfect.

I remember my reaction to the news was off the scale of normal if there is such a thing. There were no tears, no crumpled legs, in fact no hysterics. But my brain went into overdrive. I thought how stupid I was and how careless to lose the one person who loved me unconditionally. Why wasn't it me lying scrunched under a lorry on the bypass? I was the notoriously bad driver. Chris was the good guy, my hero, and the underwriter of my entire life. I remember agonising that I carried a perilous gene which courted family disaster. It was easy to recall examples to support that theory.

I had decided to do the grocery shopping on that gruesome day. We'd all been surviving on post-Christmas scraps, and I wanted to treat Chris to a red-meat feast when he came home. The house was clean from top to bottom. I'd taken the cushions off the sofa and removed the last elements of Christmas crumbs. Our bed sheets were pristine. The plan was to have the children in bed early and a bottle of red breathing on the table.

On the last day of my life as I knew it, Hannah was back at school, stroppy and spoilt from Christmas, and Tom was pre-occupied in the conservatory with a toy Father Christmas had delivered. He had yet to start school, although the big day was looming.

As the accident unfolded some twenty miles away, I'd been wrestling with the shopping list in my head. Why hadn't I felt a chill to my bones while tidying the children's bedrooms and removing a family of plastic ducks from the bath? While my soul mate lay dead on a busy main road, I dealt with the mundane chores of family life.

Chris had been an amazing father. He always tried to be home each evening for the children's bath and the flood of water across the tiles and the shrieks of childish laughter suggested they had high jinks. I always bowed to his superior knowledge about what constituted childhood fun. The children's favourite bath-game was 'slip and slide' which involved launching themselves from one end of the bath into diminishing water. Strangely, 'slip and slide' was never mentioned after Chris died; it was like the children's sacrosanct memorial to their father.

I was at the bottom of the stairs when the doorbell rang that morning. Two police officers stood there. Dumb. I say dumb because no one spoke for at least ten seconds. I broke the silence with, 'number twenty two. Your colleague lives at twenty two.' Why would police officers need directions to a colleague's home? Not the sort of mistake they'd make, I realised later. Maybe it was a defence-mechanism on my part. Anything would have been better than bad news.

But bad news it had turned out to be. A foreign lorry, loaded with steel sheets from Poland, had veered across the dual carriageway in Cheltenham and taken Chris and another car out like Matchbox toys. The driver of the lorry and the other car driver had survived. But not Chris.

Why not Chris? I was angry. No, to be precise, I was furious as hell that I had been abandoned. Why me, who only had the kids and Susie? Susie, my friend from school, was a stalwart who never gave up on me, no matter how badly I behaved. She and her husband Greg were our family, soon to become a lifeline over the coming months.

Feeling sorry for oneself is common, people told me, when trauma dumps its vicious claws into tender flesh. I wanted to scream in the street, beat-up foreigners and, at the same time, bury my head under a duvet and never come up for air.

But, of course, I did come up for air, although I didn't like what I saw. The police took me to identify Chris's body which was an alien experience. The smell, the white walls and the metal gurneys were like something out of a medical movie. I wanted to gather my darling in my arms and take him home, just to prove he wasn't dead. But he was. His cooling skin ensured there had been no mistake.

Due to my absence of family, Susie was the one who had scooped up the kids and taken them to her house. I barely remember it happening. They were left in the care of her husband, Greg.

My oh so tiny Tom thought it was a treat to share bunks with his friend Harry. Hannah decided it was an unexpected sleep-over and she and Chloe dealt with a trio of unruly dolls before eventually getting to sleep around nine.

Susie stayed with me that night and all the next day coaxing sweet tea and brandy down my throat in equal measure. We didn't tell my children about the demise of their father for twenty four hours.

Between the accident and the funeral, I'm sure life continued, if not as normal, then in some semblance of order. Greg took me to register Chris's death and Susie stayed with me day and night. She sat with me while I broke the news to the children.

The shadow of those early days still haunts me. I can still feel that hungry void in the gut and I remember Tom and Hannah crying as if they'd never stop. But being kids, they did and got their lives sorted long before I did.

The mornings were the worst time, after the children had gone to school. Usually I hadn't slept, or if I had managed a few hours, I'd woken feeling like chewed up string. Poor little Tom had his first day at school a few weeks after the accident, and I'll never shed the guilt that I allowed Susie to take him. In the early weeks, the children both arrived at the school gates courtesy of Susie, as I was nervous about driving and in no state to take responsibility for them. Left to the mercy of their mother, they would have stayed off school for weeks, gone hungry and most definitely killed each other.

'School is what they need Kate. They'll thrive on routine and being kept busy. I'll take them.'

I knew Susie was right, so Hannah and Tom made it to school each day curtesy of Aunt Susie.

'I'll collect them and give them tea each day and then bring them home. Is that OK with you? You needn't worry about anything.'

'Thank you.'

OK. I'll not worry about them. I'll let life drift over me until the reality bites me in the bum.

I did eventually get behind the wheel of my car, in the local supermarket carpark with Greg in the passenger seat and my very sweaty hands on the steering wheel. Of course I got to grips with it, for I had no option, but it was a scary time. I saw accidents waiting to happen everywhere I looked and careless foreign drivers lurking in every lorry.

Most days I'd curl up in Chris's favourite chair with a mug of coffee. Our Cotswold stone fireplace, which should have shed warmth and comfort on me, was just a pile of ash as I couldn't be assed to light it.

When the children left the house each morning I'd stare at the assortment of envelopes which had dropped through the letterbox. The mail became my enemy and if I'd had a dog, I might have set it on the postman.

A few letters were read on the day they arrived while others, particularly brown envelopes, languished on the door mat. Those I hadn't bothered to pick up, Hannah piled on the hall table when she came home. I didn't always feel up to the task of opening envelopes, especially the condolence cards. Kind words were a trigger point for tears. So, they sat in an ever-increasing pile, stared at by the wooden frame which contained our last-ever family photo.

And then there were the bills which I'd never had to deal with. As far as I could tell, most payments were on standing orders, but some were a mystery. And then the personal injury advice began plopping through the letterbox. I'd realised, of course, there would be a claim against the driver's insurance company, but the necessary process was beyond me. Next there was a bunfight of solicitors wanting to look after my interest. Letters, flyers, unwanted phone calls and doorknockers; I had no desire to sift or resist. But Greg was amazing.

'Shall I pop over each evening and help you sort the mail?'

It was an immense kindness as I knew it cut into his precious time reading bedtime stories and enjoying cuddles with his kids. But he insisted and I had no energy to argue.

So, little by little Greg and I had made sense of the paperwork. But I couldn't wring a drop of logic from the details of the accident which had changed my life in a split second of madness. I was constantly angry.

The police called a couple of times to update me on the investigation and told me the driver was insured, but drunk. They said he was way over the legal limit.

'At that time in the morning?' I remember asking the sergeant, as I made him a cup of tea.

'He was three time over the limit Mrs Roseland. He must have had vodka for breakfast, I shouldn't wonder.'

That should have put me off alcohol for life, but it didn't. I developed a liking for gin and could hardly wait for the kids to be asleep so that I could hit the bottle. It wasn't exactly a straw in a bottle affair, but very nearly.

Chapter 3

Chris had rescued Kate from an unhappy childhood, promiscuity, and poor choices in men. He'd also made her feel safer than she'd thought possible. But after the accident, with typical self-deprecation, Kate believed she had none of the essential skills to rescue her children from the trauma of losing their father. It was primarily her mindset that prevented her getting her own life back on an even keel, and there was no blueprint to assist.

'You're talking twaddle,' Susie had told her. 'You're a great mum. You put the kids before everything and they'll thrive, given time. You all will.' She was emphatic that the children would eventually find coping mechanism to move on with their lives.

Kate heard all the reasoning but had difficulty believing it. Despite her best efforts, her brain developed a constant handstand routine inside her skull. And she'd yet to grasp the reality that one careless driver had wrecked four happy lives.

Greg had given her a financial overview and although there were various claims that could take months, if not years to pay out, she knew they were solvent in the short-term. Greg shoved bits of paperwork in front of her which she signed with disinterest.

After a few weeks of personal misery, Kate marvelled at the children's ability to fight over the content of a cereal packet as if nothing had broken their lives into bits. Friends told her it was a healthy sign, proof that they were coming to terms with losing their father, as day by day they regained a normality Kate envied.

Mundane domesticity and the burden of insurance claims intruded on Kate's grieving process. She became tired of being strong, sick of coping. Sometimes she told herself a lie and just for a moment convinced herself that Chris was on a training course and would burst through the door at any minute. But it was cruel and pointless. And Kate was a realist, something she'd learnt from a young age living with Bitch-Mother. It's pointless to hide from shit if it has your name on it.

Kate had often heard Chris's voice, usually in the small hours of the morning when sleep eluded her. She'd feel the warmth of his touch, the smell of his skin. Each evening at six, she would subconsciously wait for the sound of his car on the gravel drive. She wanted to share a bottle of wine with him. Anything that was normal.

The washing pile was too small, the lavatory seat always down; no one left splashes on the bathroom mirror and the radio was silent. His toothbrush was still next to hers on the basin, and she had no idea when she'd find the strength to remove it. She'd taken to sleeping on Chris's side of the bed, curled within the place where his body had lain.

Thick mud caked Chris's walking boots on the utility room floor. Kate liked to see them there as it evoked memories of the days before he'd died. They had all wrapped up warm the day after Boxing Day and tramped through Cranham woods. They'd made trails in the leaves with branches abandoned by the winter winds. The children had run off their excess energy while she'd scuffed through the fragrant leaves with her arm linked into Chris's.

'They'll sleep tonight,' Chris said.

'You can't catch me,' Tom yelled as he dashed around a large oak tree. 'I'm Batman. Watch me Mummy. Watch me. See how fast I am. I'm flying.'

'They're not the only ones who'll sleep well,' Kate called as she'd chased Tom between the trees.

Chris had been an excellent provider. His success at GCHQ had been rewarded with various promotions and a sizeable income, and they'd enjoyed the luxury of a comfortable lifestyle. Kate had been a stay-at-home mum for the children's early years, something they'd both agreed was worth the loss of her income. Together, they had given the children all the love and security Kate had never known as a child, and they'd watched them blossom with a deep sense of satisfaction. But now, everything had changed, and it scared Kate witless.

In their son Tom, Kate saw his father's pebble-brown eyes. Amber rings were developing within the dark pools which Chris had told her resembled his late grandfather. Kate had never known Grandfer John who'd been dead for several years when she met Chris, but she took comfort from knowing that Chris's family genes lived on.

Tom, almost five and growing like a weed, threatened to outgrow his sister over the next year or so. His tawny mop of hair which was, *'one step away from a hedgehog,'* as Chris often teased, looked in constant need of brushing. But it was in Hannah that Kate saw Chris's smile, and it had a habit of snagging her heartstrings. Often, she caught a glimpse of him in her daughter's beautiful face, especially the way she frowned when logic evaded her. Small things had the ability to flip Kate's stomach and unbalance her for hours. And she found, to her shame, that she often wanted to sleep during the day. She longed to curl up like a cat on a sunny windowsill, but there were no rays of sunshine to be found.

One thing Kate had managed to do soon after Chris's death was to visit Hannah's school. She was zombie-like, brief, and tearful, but she was pleased to have made the effort. The Head agreed that Hannah would need support over the coming months, and Tom could be vulnerable when he started school in a few weeks. She'd promised Kate that she would monitor their progress.

Then there were other necessities that couldn't be avoided, such as the funeral director. Someone had booked a home visit, but she had no recollection of who had done it. Probably solid, dependable Greg.

'What colour would you like the roses? Or would you prefer lilies?' the dark suited, Uriah Heap had asked her in suitably funereal tones. 'Will the coffin bear only family flowers?'

'Why is he whispering Mummy?' Hannah watched from behind her mother's chair. 'I wish we had a granny. Ella's got a granny, and she helps when there's a lot to do.'

The image of Bitch-Mother bearing down on her grief had brought a flush to Kate's neck. Her turbulent childhood had left a residue of trauma which still lingered. But one thing she knew for sure, Bitch-Mother wasn't needed to help deal with her monumental loss.

Chris's boss had called a week after the accident, and it was a painful meeting. He'd burbled on about salary cheques and Widow's Funds which could be available to her, but Kate was pleased when he refused her offer of tea. She'd gracefully ushered him through the front door.

GCHQ management had been supportive after the accident. There had been a cash injection into her bank account, insurance policies had paid out and her mortgage was 'fully paid', as their Building Society had taken pleasure in informing her. *'Sitting pretty,'* she'd heard a neighbour whisper in the post office. Kate was used to people talking about her, they'd done it all her life.

Then came the vicar. Kate had little experience with the clergy, but this one was doing her best. 'Did Chris have a favourite hymn?' The young woman oozed empathy from her dog collar. 'A piece of music that he loved?' she'd persisted.

'I need to think about it,' Kate told her.

Susie served tea while Kate agreed to all suggestions put forward by the well-meaning lady. 'I'm afraid neither of us are...were church goers, but I know it would be important to Chris to be near his parents. They are both in the churchyard.

A church service followed by cremation was agreed, and Chris's ashes were to be brought back to the family for scattering.

Kate thought about music. After several false starts she'd decided Billy Preston's dulcet tones would be fitting; 'With You I'm Born Again.' How true that had been. But maybe it would be too painful to bear. No one had written the manual for this moment and Kate could only take advice from those closest to her.

'Follow your gut instinct Katie.' It was Greg who brought a male perspective to arrangements. 'You'll know what to do. Trust me.'

Dear Lord and Father of Mankind, Forgive Our Foolish Ways was her choice of hymn, for a reason known only to Kate.

Over the next few days Gregg had become anxious. 'Is there anyone else you can think of Kate, anyone else who needs telling? I've put the funeral arrangements in the Cheltenham Post, the Stroud News and in the Times. A lot of people will see them, but maybe some will miss it.' Gregg wanted to get things right for his friend Chris.

'That will do. Thanks.' *Do I care who comes to the funeral?*

'Would you like to give me your address book? I could browse through that if you like.'

'No. You've done more than enough Greg, thanks.'

Friends offered ready-made meals and sleepovers for the children; groceries appeared on the doorstep. "If there's anything you need," they had begged, helpless to heal the grief. But Kate had just needed the children close. She'd hugged them until they squealed and checked them a dozen times at night, to be sure they were breathing. She'd fretted when they wanted to play outside, and bike trips were banned.

Kate told herself life would eventually get back to normal, and although she knew it was a lie, it provided morsels of comfort.

Chapter 4

On the day of Chris's funeral Kate had smiled at her two small children who shone like exotic birds. They were her oasis in a desert storm. The squirrel-grey sky wielded dark clouds that threatened to burst with heavy showers. *Just how I feel*. She'd squeezed the children to her body, comforted by their warmth and thankful they were alive. They'd taken the rawness off the day.

'Can I wear my party dress?' Hannah had asked that morning. She was too young to judge funereal etiquette.

'Yes Darling. Daddy loved that dress.' Kate's throat was dry. Not to be left out, Tom announced he would wear his Batman suit. Kate had felt her eyes fill with tears but was determined the children would not see her break-down. That had been a close call.

Although neither she nor Chris had been churchgoers, it wasn't the first time she'd walked down that aisle. She'd made the same journey only seven short years before as a smiling bride on Greg's arm, so full of hope for a life of happiness with Chris.

'You'll never have to be scared again Kate. I'm going to keep you safe. No one will hurt you while I have breath in my body,' Chris had told her. *Hmm...So what about now?*

At the church door Kate had picked up strains of the organ's melancholy drone and her eyes lasered the oak coffin being wheeled before her. She absorbed the waft of incense and polished wood which inexplicably, instilled in her a deep fear for the future. As she had taken each child by the hand, she'd followed in the footsteps of every other grieving widow who'd trodden the frosty cobbles. She'd fought for breath behind the cloying scent of lilies.

'Are you both OK? We must be brave today. It's what Daddy would have wanted.'

'Don't worry Mummy. We're not babies.' Tom looked unbearably small.

As they'd walked behind the coffin like a trio of orphans, Tom had turned to his mother with a look of wonderment. 'Is Daddy really in there?' His voice echoed through the church and there wasn't a dry eye in the house. His Batman suit, almost outgrown, shed a shaft of unreality across the aisle.

It had been agreed with the vicar that she wouldn't make a eulogy. Kate couldn't imagine having the courage to stand at the lectern, only to see her fatherless children seated in the front pew. However, she had a fleeting moment of regret. Should she have had the courage to say good things about Chris? This was the first of many moments of indecision that would mar the months ahead.

After the hymn and prayers and Billy's rendering of 'With You I'm Born Again,' Tom had asked if he could put his favourite toy car on the coffin. Kate held him in her arms so that he could reach the lid.

'That's for you Daddy. It's my best one, but you can have it.'

Kate had stared at the red racing car nestled in the massive spray of lilies before leading Tom back to his seat. She'd sat him on her lap and buried her face in his tender neck, breathing deeply on the scent of small boy. She was determined not to cry.

A short service at the crematorium followed, and only close friends and family were invited. The children watched, seemingly unscathed as their daddy rolled into the furnace. His last journey on earth was scrutinised with fascination, and they were rivetted by the mechanics of the event. Hannah liked the red velvet curtains.

'They'd have been better if they were pink, but red's OK. Is somebody underneath winding that thing?'

When they arrived at the wake it was in full swing. Susie and Greg had arranged for sandwiches to be served at the local pub, and a 'first drink free policy' was organised with the Landlord. An enormous crowd had arrived, and the bar was one huge jostle of their friends and Chris's work colleagues. There was a crescendo of chatter as Kate entered with Susie, Greg and the children. Someone slipped a gin and tonic into her hand and manoeuvred her to a window seat, urging her to 'take the weight of your feet, dear.' Susie, who had brought books for the children, soon had Tom and Hannah perched on bar stools while she read to them.

People said amazing things about her husband, some stories Kate had never heard. There was the day he'd climbed on a secretary's desk to catch a spider lurking in a cobweb above her head. Chris had been liked and respected by work colleagues, and he had been an incredible husband and father.

'I can't believe some of the lovely things people are saying about Chris,' Kate said to Judy, her friend who lived four doors down.'

'Funerals always spring surprises,' her friend Emma added, as she'd squeezed past a corpulent lady who'd dusted off a felt hat for the occasion. 'At least he wasn't screwing a blonde bimbo who'd wailed from the back pew.'

Kate had smiled despite her overpowering grief. Emma was a solicitor and never pulled her punches. Kate loved her for it. Not married, Emma represented the militant strand of the girls who'd shared their years at High School. They'd all survived its traumas during their teenaged years, but Emma had orchestrated more than one divorce within the group.

'Chris was truly a wonderful man.' Poppy, her cherished, next-door neighbour appeared grasping a pint glass of orange juice.

'Yes, he was Poppy. I have no idea how we are going to live without him.'

Kate spotted a tall, commanding woman bearing down with a large glass of wine in her manicured hand. 'I want to give you a big hug Kate. And haven't your babies grown into adorable children?' It was Penny, the wife of the local estate agent who was given to gushing. Kate endured the proffered tight squeeze but would have preferred her not to bother. 'You were so brave during the service Kate. I'm full of admiration for you.'

Susie came to the rescue. 'I've left Molly Saunders with the children. She's found some crayons and they're creating a zoo on the back of the pub menus.' She stood next to Kate without acknowledging Penny who drifted away like a bad smell. 'I never liked that insensitive cow. I'm surprised she didn't weep all over you and tell you her marital problems.' Susie's views were not to be denied, even at a funeral.

'Never could understand what she and Bob had in common. But people probably say that about Chris and me.' Kate was already wishing everyone would go home.

'Chris adored you and everyone knows it. Not today, Katie. Don't put yourself down today. You're doing an amazing job and Chris would have been so proud of you.'

Kate gulped. Another close call.

'I'm going to get you another gin Darling. Don't move and don't talk to anyone 'til I get back. Stick with her Em. Guard her with your life.'

Kate had watched the crowd like an outsider who didn't belong; she was that teenager again who never quite fitted in. No matter how many accolades were paid to Chris, how much sympathy was voiced, she couldn't find a strand of reality about the day.

Poppy reappeared like a fairy godmother and put an arm on her shoulder.

'Shall I take the children home for you Kate? I could give them tea and you wouldn't have to worry about how long you stay here.'

Kate had hesitated. She'd rather be anywhere else right now, but she knew duty called.

'I'm sure there must be people who would love to speak with you,' Poppy had encouraged.

'That's right. You haven't had much chance to speak to anyone.' Emma was in favour. 'They'll expect it.'

Kate contemplated Poppy's kind gesture. 'I'll ask them,' she said. 'Thank you, Poppy.'

Ten minutes later, as Poppy had taken each child by the hand and led them out of the pub, neither had given Kate a backward glance.

Emma said, 'Kids, eh? You are grieving your heart out and they wander off without a care in the world. It's bound to hit them later but for the moment, it doesn't look as if you need to worry too much.'

Kate had felt a cold gush of reality as she'd watched the children disappear. It was almost a panic attack, a shortness of breath, a loss of words. She'd allowed her children to be taken away. What would Chris have thought? But she had reasoned herself back into the moment. The vicar needed thanking and she must find Chris's godmother, Juliet, who'd been a mainstay to his family. She had responsibilities and this was no place for drama-queens.

Eventually it was over.

Life settled into an unstable routine that was likely to crumble at the slightest hiccup. The food cupboard was filled for the moment, the dustbins were emptied on the appropriate day, and the piles of washing usually made it into the machine. But nothing was guaranteed.

Susie, however, was a constant. 'You need to get a grip around the kids,' she'd told Kate during a trip to Tesco. 'I know the grief is still raw for you, and understandably so, but really, kids are resilient.' Susie piled her trolley with teabags, coffee, and sugar-substitute from the shelves. 'They're bouncing back, and you haven't noticed,' she continued. 'They need to get their routines sorted. They need to get out more.'

Kate had burst into tears. She wasn't ready for Susie's brutal words, even though they carried a ring of truth. 'Knowing the answers and acting on them are two different things.' Kate searched out a tissue to catch the tears. 'I'm trying to cope. Really, I am, but it's bloody hard.'

'I know Katie. I know. But if I don't step in with a guiding hand, who's going to? You are a bit of an Orphan-Annie!'

Kate had managed a smile. She knew her blunt, but treasured friend was right. It had taken a quick mopping-up operation before they moved into the cereal aisle.

'You could have counselling,' Susie said, more gently, pausing at the Cornflakes. 'Why not join a group? It might help to sort out your head and meeting others who know how you feel, that could be good.'

Kate had forgotten Rice Krispies and abandoned her trolley to retrieve them. 'I hope this is the packet with stickers inside. There'll be hell to pay if I get it wrong.'

But Susie wasn't easily distracted. 'You've been through a massive shock and it's no wonder you're off-kilter, Kate.' She grabbed two tins of baked beans and some tuna.

'You make me feel like a head-case.' Kate had busied herself amongst the olive oil and fought another onslaught of tears.

'You know I don't mean that. How you feel is natural Katie and no one can begin to understand unless they've been there. You're grieving, but you have a family to cope with while you're doing it. I know it must be hellishly difficult.'

Susie had marched with intent upon the cooking ingredients before her next offering. 'But it hurts to see you like this. You're as jumpy as our new kitten and she's only six weeks old.' She'd placed an arm around Kate. 'Be kind to yourself for a change. Have you tried this Harvest Bake?'

Susie was a good hugger and for a split second, beside the dried fruit, her arms had made Kate feel safe.

But Kate didn't consider counselling. *Counselling is for wimps*. And anyway, she knew how to rise above personal disaster. Hadn't she done it for most of her childhood? She could probably write the textbook on grief, and she'd certainly got the tee-shirt. And anyway, as she told herself every day, she'd cope in her own time. But she had to admit she was in danger of choking the children on an ever-shortened leash. Susie was right. She hadn't even allowed them to watch the carnival glide through the streets of the local town for fear of.... what? A flying clown disaster? *Yeah right*.

It took Kate almost a year to sort Chris's clothes and belongings. She'd sat day after day on their bed, staring at the open wardrobes, fearing the scent of him would tip her over the edge.

'Why don't you let me take some clothes to a charity shop?' Susie was well-meaning and it had already been four months since Chris had died, but it was something Kate needed to do herself. When she was ready. Sometimes she took comfort from his jumpers and wallowed in the aroma of a man now dead. One day, she had taken Chris's navy wool coat off its hanger and snuggled it around her shoulders. It felt cosy and it felt safe. It was a place to lose herself, a place where the world couldn't make demands on her.

A mum from Kate's yoga class spoke to her at the school gate and assured her that one day she'd wake up and realise that life was worth living again. 'It took me more than a year after Jeff finally succumbed to cancer,' she'd told Kate. 'Most of the time I didn't even know what day of the week it was. But believe me, things do get better.'

I'll look forward to that, then.

Kate hadn't needed to be told that she'd changed, both mentally and physically. She'd lost weight, she forgot things, sometimes important things, and was too tired to have opinions about anything. Her previous, bubbly personality and bold take on life had gone missing. It was as if the old Kate had slithered down a black hole, leaving only her skeleton in the real world.

Despite every effort to desist, she obsessed over the image of Chris's mangled body being ripped from the sardine can that had once been his car. She imagined him being carried by strangers to the indifference of the Cheltenham morgue, and all before she'd had chance to say goodbye. He'd been 'swabbed down' and 'cleaned up' by hands that neither knew nor cared about him. And it had felt an injustice, an invasion of privacy and yes, it was life changing.

And then, one day, months after the accident, Kate hauled an armful of hangers and tossed them, clothes and all, into the boot of her car. She felt guilty about her lack of respect. Surely, she should have folded them neatly, made some semblance of order from the chaos. But she couldn't. *I don't care which charity has them as long as it's not the bloody Care for Pets in Barnard Street.*

Bitch-Mother had loved animals more than a small, adopted girl and it had left its mark on Kate; it left her with a loathing for cats and small dogs, especially those with ribbon tied in a topknot. Not that she would hurt a dog, but she preferred to stay away from them and certainly didn't want Chris's clothes to aid the yappy little bastards. She decided upon the Salvation Army. Yes. That's what she'd do with them and there was space to park outside the shop, too. The job wasn't finished, it wasn't even half done, but it was a good start.

If everyday life was hard, Kate had found holidays excruciatingly difficult, too. *How can you celebrate when the kids have no daddy to share chocolate eggs, eat birthday cake or to buy a present for Mummy?* And that first summer after Chris's death, they'd had days out rather than a proper holiday. The Isles of Scilly held no appeal as a single parent. There were too many happy memories spent as a family, lingering in the freezing blue water, and picnicking on white sandy beaches. It had been Chris's favourite place on earth.

Eventually, Kate had survived the first anniversary of Chris's death, the first Christmas without him and three family birthdays. She'd read textbooks on grief, but still nothing ousted the terrors that haunted her. She saw tangled metal and ambulances where there was only a children's playpark, and every noise made her jump. She knew she needed to get a hold on her life. It was time to start living again. Kate had never been a wimp, but hard as she tried, she couldn't unearth any semblance of her old self from the dross that now marred her life. And her mood was beginning to affect the children.

Chapter 5

Kate

I learnt to push boundaries at a young age and the mundane in life has never been enough for me. My life with Bitch-Mother taught me to lie with compunction and evade her beatings by stealth. Nothing I did or achieved ever satisfied her or brought forth the slightest sign of approval hence my concept of what constituted family life was so far of the radar of normal that I was a danger to myself. Eventually, by the time I was twelve, by life consisted of defence tactics to conserve my sanity.

I suppose in my adult years, before Chris, I was a thrill-seeker although, strangely, I didn't have any desire to experiment with boys in my adolescence. I was a late developer, having been warned of the ghastliness of 'all that sex business' by Bitch-Mother when I was about twelve. "Don't bother your head with sex Katherine. It's not what it's cracked up to be, believe me."

That was my sex education, given in one sentence by a woman who had adopted a child rather than risk the 'messy process of childbirth.' The rest of it I'd learnt at school, but my interest in experimenting was absent due to an unproportionate fear of getting pregnant.

The first time I was beaten by the witch was when I was a frightened little girl of five being passed from one family to another but with no explanation of my fate. The last time Bitch-Mother laid a disciplining hand on me was two days before my eighteenth birthday. I'd disobeyed her order not to go to Youth Club and had sneaked out with hairspray and lipstick which I applied as I walked into the village. I'd thought little about the consequences, although I'd known they would be harsh.

She'd caught me unaware when I returned home. As I'd bent to remove my shoes in the doorway, a spectacular punch landed on my nose. It created a spurt of blood which I was unable to contain in a handkerchief, so I'd stood at the kitchen sink and bled down the plughole. That was the final act of cruelty needed for me to make up my mind. I had to get out.

Many ideas filled my young head, mostly based on a desire to be loved and wanted. Neither of which were forthcoming from my useless parents. As the result of a loveless childhood, I promised myself that one day I'd search for my birthmother. She who had given me life and for whatever reason set me loose on a tide of misery. I'd convinced myself she couldn't be more of a monster than Bitch-Mother, or could she? Whatever the outcome, it would be many years before I found the courage to begin my search.

I was allowed to take up a nursing career, probably because my parents were pleased to see the back of me, and I was certainly anxious to get out of their reach. So, at eighteen I joined a bevy of trainee-nurses in Bristol. We had all arrived at the training school fresh-faced and eager, and each with her own agenda. Many had wanted a medical man to marry while for some, it was a professional career driven by ambition. For me it was escape from the dysfunctional cow I called Bitch-Mother.

The photographs of my teenaged years suggest I was pretty enough, but having not one jot of self-confidence, I never acknowledged it. I was tall and willowy with a thatch of unruly auburn curls, a cute turned up nose and a creamy skin which, to my annoyance, was given to an abundance of summer freckles.

I was never without male attention from the age of fourteen, but I rebuffed all advances until I left home. By then, I suspect I wore a flashing beacon on my head or had 'needy' tattooed on my forehead. I'd been desperate for kindness and love, but when they arrived, I misinterpreted them and found men could lead you down dangerous paths. *If they want to sleep with me then they must love me. Mustn't they?* Mine was an open heart waiting to be trampled upon.

Bristol harboured an excess of men to choose from; dental students, medical students, language buffs and scientists were all single and looking for fun. It had felt as if Bristol was a city of excesses, and I'd been determined to make up for lost time. Small town life and Bitch-Mother felt a million miles away. I would never speak to her again or set foot in her home.

After an eight week spell in the classroom, we student nurses were let onto the wards for practical training on real patients. It had mostly involved emptying bedpans, scrubbing beds, and running errands during the first year, but I told myself it was the start of something that would give me freedom and independence. I persuaded a doctor to put me on the pill as the last thing I wanted was an un-planned pregnancy.

There was fun to be had in fashion and dancing; I wore long tartan skirts or short skirts closely resembling wide belts and discovered black eyeliner and perfume. I straightened my unruly curls to within an inch of their lives and when in my nurse's uniform I stretched them into a bun that sat neatly within my starched white cap. Oh how proud we nurses were of our uniforms.

Nursing really suited me which was more by luck than any planning. I knew I had to make a success of it as there would be no going back. My bridges were well and truly burned.

I think it was the camaraderie of the girls, my work with patients and the freedom to go to parties and nightclubs that enthralled me. The rules we lived by were strict although they bore no resemblance to my upbringing. Each nurse had two late passes until midnight, and every other night she had to be in by ten thirty. No wonder we became adept at climbing drainpipes and keeping ground floor windows unlocked.

The nurse's home phone-booth was always packed with invitations to parties in the University Halls of Residence. A group of us often walked to Clifton and over the suspension bridge where we marvelled at the sludge and a tide that rarely appeared to cover it. I remember our reluctance to wear coats led to many chilly blasts around the thighs. But the party was always the best and the men the sexiest in town.

I was delighted when Susie decided to make Bristol her training ground for teaching. Although she lived on the other side of the city, we often spent time together, especially on the days I worked a split-shift. I envied her the long college holidays when she travelled to Europe and generally lazed around, while I was working my backside off looking after sick people under the draconian eye of ward sister. But I was determined to last the course; I knew that qualification was the key to my future.

During the first year I'd burned the candle at both ends and only just passed my exams. There was a stern talking-to from Matron who told me to "spend more time on nursing and less on boys." Not much got past her. But I'd been blessed with the ability to cram my notes just a few days before exams and only needed to forgo a week away from the high life.

It was during my second year that I'd had my first fling with a married man. In defence, I didn't choose him, he chose me. He was a police officer I'd met while on night duty. The randy, attractive man and his sidekick who wasn't worth a second look, had a habit of making the nurse's canteen their tea stop. And always when the nurses had lunch at about one in the morning. It was probably the uniform that held my interest. That, his charming line in corny jokes, and the compliments he paid me. I wasn't too familiar with compliments, and it was a good feeling to be singled out from the other nurses. He didn't mention his unavailability until the relationship was into its third month. It was the night-cook who took me to one side and spilled the beans.

'He's a nice enough guy but he's been through hordes of young nurses, and he's married.'

Whoops. Luckily for me, my night-duty came to an end, and I extricated myself before it was too late.

Susie met Greg around this time, and they quickly resembled an old married couple. They tried to fix me up with 'suitable' guys but 'suitable' always turned out to be boring. Susie told me my moral compass was adrift and she was right. It would be several years before I'd correct it and then only by a few degrees. And not before I'd damaged a few men and myself as well.

Ash was the one who got away. I often thought back on that time and decided it was premature timing when he appeared in my life. If it had been a year later, things could have been different. He was a pig farmer, although he never smelled like one. Tall, blonde, and handsome in a quirky, out-doors kind of way he was kind and good fun to be with.

We'd met at a bar in the centre of Bristol when I was out with some drippy under-graduate who'd thought he'd rivet me with a blow by blow account of his thesis on 'the effect of the common cold on Pygmies.' I'd ditched him when Ash gave me the eye from across the bar. It was the usual trick; I told Drip I was going to the loo, freshened my lipstick and slipped to the other side of the bar and accepted a drink from Ash.

Ash was the eldest son of a family of five who farmed land around Chew Magna. His two sisters were uninterested in the farm, and it was accepted that Ash would take over the business at some time in the future. I'd loved his family. The best times were when I had an invitation to Sunday lunch and lingered in the fragrance of the family kitchen. It took a lot of wheeling and dealing of the rota sheets to get a Sunday off, but when I was lucky, Ash would meet me around ten in the morning and take me home to his family. When we arrived, he'd leave me with his Mum, Alison, while he fed the pigs. I'd peel potatoes, tell her about life on the wards and not only pick up tips on how to cook, but learnt what proper family life could be. Looking back, I'm sure they assumed I'd be a farmer's wife when I qualified as a nurse.

And for a while, I was off the market. I didn't even look at other men for six months. Ash and Greg got along well, and we double-dated to balls and bars, clubs, and casinos, mostly paid for by the guys as Susie and I were paupers.

'Thank God you've found a little gem Katie. Hold on to Ash. He's a keeper,' Susie had encouraged.

But I didn't and he wasn't. I'd kicked against everyone's assumptions that I'd become a pig farmer's domestic Goddess. Or even a pig farmer's wife. I have no idea why, except that I'd felt pressured to conform and I hadn't done any living. No travelling and, I suppose, not enough playing around. Perhaps I was too immature to settle down.

Eventually, after nursing a broken heart brought about by my bad behaviour, Ash met a vet who not only deserved him, but gave him a strapping son, a baby daughter and free treatment for his pigs. I love happy endings.

Even now, years later, Susie occasionally mentions Ash. She uses her schoolteacher's slightly critical tone which rarely intimidates me. "I did it my way," I frequently told her, although I know her disapproval of my treatment of Ash lives on. She couldn't believe my foolhardiness and I think she and Greg still see him from time to time. Susie brings snippets of information about any new arrival, babies not pigs, and she also told me when Alison died of breast cancer. That made me sad.

So, having broken Ash's heart in the heat of August, I'd turned my interest to the new intake of medics arriving in the hospital. It was here I met Simon. Black-haired, melting-toffee-eyed Simon. Having ditched a loving farmer, I exchanged him for a bastard doctor who treated me badly and then threw me to the wolves.

During my student nurse years, I'd learned to appreciate a new way of life. One I had no idea existed. I enjoyed fun, freedom, men, who came in all shapes and sizes, dancing, friendships, and most of all, independence. Money was always tight, but Susie and I used to search the charity shops for items we could adapt. This usually involved shortening and taking in seams until we gasped for breath. We both revelled in the glamorous, heady mix of pop-culture and given the chance, we would have been one of the screaming mob of girls who followed their idols.

About eighteen months after saying goodbye to Ash, my lovely Chris appeared. I met him at a friend's party in Cheltenham, about eight weeks prior to my finals. I was cramming hard to make the grade.

The party was dull, and I'd been sitting on an open window-ledge with a can of beer, thinking I should be swatting instead of moping about. Chris had crept up beside me, grabbed me as if to push me out of the window, and then laughed that he'd scared me.

'Sensible girls don't sit in window-ledges. Especially three floors up.'

'Good job I'm not sensible.'

'Ah. Red haired and fiery.'

'Something like that.'

And so, it began. I was impressed that he worked at GCHQ but bloody irritated that he'd never talk about his work. He became my very own James Bond and wooed me in an old-fashioned way. Flowers arrived at the nurse's home the day before my finals; he'd open doors for me with not a hint of embarrassment and was ultra-sensitive when we started sleeping together. He was a novelty for me. Kind, good-looking and stable. What did he see in a fiery, red-headed nurse?

But it became clear he really wanted me, and he wanted me exactly as I was, warts and all. I wasn't familiar or comfortable with being wanted, even at the age of twenty one. Naivety and wantonness ran through me like a stick of rock. Not easy bedfellows, as Susie had told me on more than one occasion. I found it easy, however, to regale the story of my life to Chris. I didn't want any secrets festering, just waiting to be discovered.

Chris had no close family either. His parents had died in a terrible car crash when he was in his teens, and his godmother was the closest he had to a family. I'd met Juliet shortly after our first date when I'd been shown off to her with pride as, 'the girl I'm going to marry'. Despite the trauma of his early years when he was packed off to boarding school, Chris was surprisingly well-balanced. He'd claimed he had his mother's intelligence and his father's looks, a combination that satisfied me, at least for the time being. I'd decided the loss of his parents at a young age was a tenuous bond between us. He'd understood my loneliness and the yearning that never quite became the spoken word. Being with Chris felt right. We fitted together.

Chapter 6

After qualifying Kate took a staff nurse post at Southmead Hospital on the north side of Bristol. This made meeting up with Chris easier. Theirs was a run-of-the mill courtship with no firecrackers or moments of high-passion. But it was calm and safe, and Chris had convinced her he could heal her childhood damage.

Kate knew Chris was her chance to settle down and be loved unreservedly. It had felt different from Ash. She'd acquired more life experience, enjoyed plenty of fun, but most crucially, she'd learnt from her mistakes. Or so she believed. And then, of course, she'd had Susie's encouragement in her ear.

So, Kate made a list of pros and cons about the decision to marry Chris, which didn't feel a very romantic approach to marriage, but had some merit. She'd discovered she could only write 'slightly boring' in the cons list; the pros on the other hand included things like 'good father material', 'kind', 'steady,' and 'reliable'. Hmm....

'For God's sake Kate. Don't let another good one slip through your fingers. Why do you only want the bastards?'

'Just so that you know, Susie Clever Clogs, I'm giving it serious consideration.

'Alleluia.'

And so, after a gentle year of courtship, she had married Chris. It was a quiet affair with Susie as her bridesmaid and parents missing on both sides.

Kate was faithful to Chris for almost a year, and she'd claimed her first misdemeanour wasn't entirely her fault. The perpetrator was a porter in the hospital who was tall and good-looking and who'd become a regular visitor to the men's surgical ward. Even on days when there were no surgical lists. He'd appear when Kate was checking meds or in the office updating the Kardex. One day he saw her in town and had the audacity to whisper in her ear all the things he wanted to do to her. Kate admitted to her friend Julie that she'd not discouraged him, although she should have.

One quiet afternoon when Sister was off duty, the handsome porter had pounced on Kate in the ward kitchen as she'd been boiling milk for a patient's Complan. Before she could draw breath, she was shoved in the broom cupboard with her skirt up around her waist and adrenalin rising even higher. His lips had enclosed her like suction pads and his expert hands made her moan. It was over in four urgent minutes, and she'd managed to exit the cupboard with her professional dignity intact, and Mr. Smyth's Complan not yet cool.

'Uniforms do it for me every time,' he'd told her with a cheeky wink. And then he'd whistled his way down the ward and out into the corridor.

'Nice looking young buck,' said old Mr Wiltshire. 'Bet he's got his eye on a young nurse.'

'Well, he'd better not look my way,' Kate managed as she disappeared into the staff loo to sort herself out.

She should have reported him to Matron, of course, but he had such a disarming smile and a cock like an elephant.

'Not that I'm conversant with elephant's willies, but you get the gist,' she'd later told Susie. 'Is there anything more exciting than a lustful fuck in a broom cupboard?'

Susie was almost dumb struck when she'd heard. 'Why the hell would you risk your marriage, you prat?'

'How can a quickie in the hospital broom cupboard risk my marriage? Don't be a drama-queen Susie.'

'I give up Kate. But do it. If it's what you want. You must need your head read, that's all I'm saying.'

'A bit dramatic even for you.'

'Dramatic? What am I supposed to do with the information? Not tell my husband. Not tell yours. I have to carry your grubby little secret. I can't pretend it didn't happen. Thanks for that.'

It was a week before she rang Kate again.

Kate discovered the attractive porter was called Liam; a *'failure at school and devoid of life-skills'* Liam, to be exact. Married Liam to be even more exact. And although he'd fucked like a rabbit, Kate took Susie's advice and vowed to be faithful to Chris from that day on. Eventually Liam lost his job, probably because he was never where he should be at any given time. Kate later heard on the grapevine that Sister had enjoyed his charms, too.

Chris and Kate bought a house in Thornbury which was an excellent compromise on their journeys to work. Each morning, they'd head off in different directions but neither had too far to travel. Kate job-shared with a nurse who had small children and could only work weekends. It was perfect. Not exactly nine to five, but good hours by nursing standards.

Chris entered fully into the spirit of married life. They'd shopped for groceries together, tackled the laundry and the garden in tandem, and made friends with a bunch of young people who used the William's Arms which was just down the road. Life should have been perfect, but is it ever perfect?

One day Kate took a patient with a burst appendix to theatre for surgery. It was an unusual role for a senior nurse, but the ward had been short staffed. She'd wheeled the trolley along the corridor and pushed open the swinging steel doors into the anaesthetic room. Immediately she'd caught a drift of aftershave and an eyeful of the new anaesthetist. Dr Jarvis was beautiful. Not handsome, but truly beautiful. The dark hair was just visible under his scrub cap, but nothing clouded his bluebell eyes, perfect nose, or rosebud lips. And then he smiled.

'Shall I take Mr Harris from here, Staff?'

Kate must have gawped because a theatre nurse had nudged her aside and taken charge of the trolley.

'Of course...Sorry. Yes.'

Kate didn't see Ned Jarvis for at least three weeks after that first sighting. But one evening when she came off shift, she'd popped into the local convenience store to buy something for supper. And there he was, lurking behind the baked beans.

'You know what happens if you eat too many baked beans,' she'd quipped. Colour had risen in her cheeks due to the unexpected encounter.

'Is there anything else a bachelor can do with beans? I've made them into a stew, put mashed spuds on top and mixed them with cheese. My imagination fails me at that point.'

'Sounds like you need cookery lessons from an expert,' she'd replied.

'Then we should sync our diaries, don't you think?'

Kate was about to make a sassy retort when she remembered her vow of faithfulness to Chris. 'Sorry,' she said, waving her wedding ring at him. 'Married you see.'

'Just my luck. Hope he knows what a lucky guy he is.'

'I make sure of it,' Kate said with a smile.

Chapter 7

Kate

Guilt has become a recurring theme for me. Firstly, guilt about our fatherless children who deserve better, and then the guilt that I never fully appreciated Chris's generosity and love until he was gone. And why had Chris never felt totally fulfilling? After he died, I beat myself up in the most brutal way, and concluded I was profoundly damaged. Deeply, deeply damaged. Maybe I would never be totally committed to any guy for the rest of my life.

'Picking up guys comes too easily to you. That's the problem. Just be sure you put them down before any harm is done.' Susie is a great analyser and she find's my life an irresistible blank canvas. 'If you had to work a bit harder at getting fellas, you might think a bit more of the consequences.

Ouch!

But she was right. Mere eye contact with a sexy guy had the ability to land me in trouble. Something I'd avoided since the mistake with 'no skills Liam'. When I look back at that time, I'm appalled at my behaviour but I have to live with it. Not only was the HIV virus a risk, but Chris would have been devastated had he found out. He knew all about my past, my insecurities and promiscuity. But he was head over heels in love with me and convinced that his love gave me everything I needed. I wasn't totally convinced about that, although he'd swept me along in a haze of love which was infectious. He met with approval from my friends who told me he "was just what I needed." Everyone can't be wrong.

When Chris and I started talking about having a family, I was overjoyed. At last, I would have a human being who was blood related and this little being would know its parentage. For me, that personal issue had gnawed away for as long as I could remember, and the void created by not knowing where I came from was a constant snag on my heart.

Finding a larger home was a decision we took immediately we discovered Hannah was on the way, and it was agreed I'd give up work. We moved to a sleepy Cotswold village not too far from my childhood home but, more importantly, close to Susie and Greg. It was an easy commute to work for Chris and an area he, too, knew well.

'Are you sure you're not digging up the past if we move so close to your parents? Chris had expressed concern about my happiness.

'I think it will be healthy. Anyway, I don't consider them my parents.'

'But you might see them around. Can you handle that.'

'No problem. If anything, it will prove I'm over Bitch-Mother. And I really love the house. Let's do it.'

So, we moved into our dream house and at my request, its proximity to Bitch-Mother didn't enter the equation.

Our next door neighbour had called on us a couple of days after we'd moved in. She'd baked a lemon drizzle cake to welcome us and the citrus aroma insisted we eat it immediately. Chris made a pot of tea.

'Call me Poppy,' she'd told us. And don't be afraid to ask if you want a baby-sitter,' she'd added, acknowledging my seven month bump. I'd be only too happy, once you've got to know me, of course'. She'd smiled. 'I used to be a nurse.'

Poppy and I had immediate chemistry. She was two generations older than me, but it didn't show. We talked nursing and village matters, and when we had the house as we wanted it and had time to breath, we invited her to supper.

A friendship grew between us, and I discovered living next door to Poppy suited not only Chris and me. There was a vacancy in the grandchild generation waiting to be filled in Poppy's house, and she waited with bated breath for Hannah to arrive.

When I squeezed my firstborn into the world, I thought my life was complete. I'd peeped at the red-faced infant cocooned in a white blanket and met, for the first time, someone who belonged to me. I'd marvelled in the moment as I'd never known a blood relative, and Hannah was my own little miracle.

'Look at her perfect nails Kate. Can you believe it? We made her.'

'Look at her perfect everything. She's ours Chris. Aren't we lucky?' I hadn't been able to resist caressing a tiny human being who belonged to me. In old fashioned jargon, my heart swelled with gratitude for Chris, who not only loved me, but had helped me make this precious gift.

Life ambled along in a haze of happiness. I met other mothers at antenatal classes and our social life blossomed. Susie and Greg were always up for a pub meal or a trip to the theatre. We found ourselves part of a group of young marrieds, who not only had much in common, but injected humour and friendship into our lives.

True to her word Poppy loved to babysit and we felt totally confident leaving our firstborn in her care. As soon as I had weaned Hannah onto a bottle, we found freedom to enjoy seeing friends.

'She's a little gem. Your Hannah.'

'Yes, she is Poppy, although I'll bet she'll be a handful when she hits puberty!'

Then came Tom. A bigger baby than Hannah had been, and he left his mark on my nether regions. But could life have been any more perfect? I knew I was privileged to be a stay at home mother, although it wasn't the easy ride some may have thought. Hannah was a little minx. She took double my time and I often found little Tom, who was so content, was getting short shrift. I don't believe he noticed, but I did.

Poppy saw only the good in both our children and they adored her. When Tom arrived, we had worried that babysitting two children may have been a bit much for her. However, provided they were both in bed before we went out, she'd insisted there were no problems. Lucky us. She doted on both of our children and watched their development with a keen interest. And they both gave unconditional love to our neighbour.

Poppy was invaluable when Chris died. Always on call at any time of the day or night. One day, she told me about something that had happened to her when she was a young woman.

'I was engaged to be married when I was eighteen.'

She'd paused. Maybe she was weighing the suitability of what she was about to tell a grieving widow. Or maybe the emotion was still raw after decades had passed.

'He was killed right at the end of the war. He was two days from coming home.' Tears glistened as she recalled the pain.

'Oh Poppy.' I hugged her to me, and we cried in each other's arms. We had yet another experience in common.

As the children grew, they often spent time in Poppy's house which, they insisted, was far more interesting than ours.

'Why don't *we* have a box of treasures? Poppy's house is much more fun than ours.' Hannah was always after new pastimes.

'Maybe you should make your own. I can find you a shoebox if you like. I had treasures when I was young.'

Hannah and Tom asked Poppy for advice about finding treasures, and the next few weeks had seen a hive of activity while they searched and found the weird and wonderful.

'Do you think I should put Bobby in the box?' Hannah's bedraggled panda rarely left her bed.

'Why don't you try it for a night or two? If you miss him, he can come back onto your bed.'

He stayed in the box.

Poppy tended to spoil the children, often with sweets and money to spend at the shops. I tried to keep an eye on things, and often insisted any money they received was posted into their moneyboxes. Sometimes Poppy allowed Hannah to enjoy the contents of her jewellery box, which displayed countless treasures to fascinate a small girl.

'Be sure you're careful with Poppy's precious things,' I reminded her frequently.

Poppy allowed Hannah to pin a flower brooch to her dress or marvel at a mysterious diamond ring. Sometimes Hannah came home with a gift.

'Poppy says I can keep it. She says I'm just like the little girl she wished she'd had. Is Poppy sad, Mummy?'

'No Darling. She isn't sad, but sometimes people love small children very much. Aren't you lucky?'

Tom always preferred the collection of china dogs kept in a glass cabinet. He was allowed to take them out for inspection, provided they were placed on the kitchen table for safety. One afternoon he came home with the ugliest Pug dog I had ever seen.

'Poppy said I could choose. Do you think I chose the best one Mummy?'

'I do. What a good choice. Will he have a name?'

'What do you think Daddy would have called him?'

Shit. Why do I still get a wobble after all this time? 'If we'd ever had a real dog Daddy wanted to call him Toby. How about that?'

'Toby. I like Toby.'

So, Toby came to live with us.

'Poppy is like a grandma, isn't she? I've always wanted a grandma.'

'She is Darling.' I'd felt a knot in my heart when the children highlighted another thing I'd failed to provide for them.

Chapter 8

Kate

The time I remember as most difficult to handle when we lost Chris was our first Christmas without him. I'd tried to pretend Christmas wasn't happening. I ignored the television commercials, I didn't even see the lights around the town, and it wasn't until the children's Christmas diary arrived in their homework bags, that I had to face the coming of the festive season.

<u>Nativity:</u> please provide a tea towel and dressing gown. <u>Carol Service:</u> two tickets per family will be issued due to lack of space. <u>Christmas Party:</u> please provide a plate of savoury/sweet food to be brought before 3.15pm on the day.

I could no longer ignore it.

I'd shopped for the children and for Susie's family in a fog of emotion. Every gift I'd chosen was purchased in a slush of unreality. I bought a silk scarf for Juliette and patted myself on the back for not only remembering her, but for posting it in time for a Christmas arrival. Chris's lovely Godmother rang and invited us to stay for Christmas, but I made an excuse, telling her the children needed to be at home. Susie had invited us to be with them long before December arrived, but I'd delayed any decision.

A couple of weeks before the big day Susie rang me. 'Just so that you know, you're coming to us for Christmas. You'll have to cope with Greg's mother who refuses to wear her hearing aid and can be tedious. The upside is, we can talk about her, and she hasn't a clue.'

'Not half as tedious as I'll be. And I'll hear you if you talk about me.'

Greg's mother lived in an annex attached to their beautiful Cotswold stone house. I knew she irritated Susie at times, but I always found Murial easy to talk to and certainly not an overbearing sort. Maybe Susie wore the trousers a little too tight to accommodate Murial.

Eventually, I'd decided it would be great for the kids to be with our closest friends. Not because the only alternative was three of us playing at Christmas in our own house, but the children always felt safe at Susie's and our first Christmas without Chris was bound to be a tricky time for us all. In addition, Susie is a superb cook and Greg likes a tipple, so all in all, their kind invitation was the best chance for us to get the first Christmas behind us.

I'd got the decorations out of the roof space and left the boxes unopened until the children came home from school.

'Shall we put up decorations? What do you think?'

'Yes. Let's do it now.' Tom was right on top of it, opening boxes and pulling tinsel and decorations from where his father had so lovingly placed them last year. I could hardly bear to look. I could smell Chris; I could hear his laughter and it plucked at my heart.

We spent a happy time decorating the tree and all was well until the lights refused to glow.

'Daddy would have fixed them,' said Hannah. 'You don't know what to do. Do you?' With that little gem she'd burst into tears.

No. I bloody well don't, but how hard can it be?

I gave Hannah a cuddle and took comfort from her warmth. My little girl was uttering words she should never have to say. 'I think we should check the bulbs are all in tight. It's something like that.'

'I know. I know what to do. Daddy always let me help him and they never worked unless you fiddled with them.'

My small son made my eyes fill with tears. *Pull yourself together. Fiddle with them.* And fiddling worked. Ever since that first Christmas, it's become standard practice to fiddle with the tree lights.

We were all transformed when the tree burst into light. Tears were forgotten as Hannah insisted on spraying snow from a can onto every branch. All Tom wanted was to know where the presents were. Sadly, he'd learnt about the lies adults tell and knew I was his source of gifts. I always had to buy extra for them as we were Johny No Mates when it came to family.

Tom announced he wanted snow for Christmas, the same thing he wanted every year.

'Daddy always said it never snows at Christmas, but do you think it might snow this year, Mummy?' His nose was pressed against the window, willing the dark sky to yield to his desire.

'It might. You never know when it's going to snow, so why not this Christmas?'

The children were enthusiastic about spending Christmas Day with Susie's kids, Chloe and Harry. They'd known each other from birth and for me, in the absence of a husband, it was natural to be with Susie and Greg.

Sometimes it felt as if my children were immune to the absence of their father. If they missed him, they didn't mention it. Greg was so lovely with them and divided his time equally between the four children. Train tracks and mechanical cars mingled with annuals and family games. The content of the Christmas crackers held as much interest for the children as expensive toys. Isn't that often the way?

When the adults were stuffed with turkey and red wine, to appease the kids we were tolerating One Hundred and One Dalmatians. The children were on the edge of fractious, mostly due to a sugar high from selection boxes, already half eaten. Harry was sprawled across his father's lap, Tom was lying on the floor at my feet, and Hannah and Chloe were together on a sofa. Suddenly Tom stood up, trampling on my feet in the process and lunged at Harry, using all his strength to beat him about the head.

'Woah Tiger.' Greg held an arm to protect his son from the onslaught of my five year old.

'Tom. What on earth do you think you're doing?' I moved quicker than a sand snake to prevent him hurting little Harry who looked dazed. 'Stop that right now.'

I pulled my son from the disaster zone with a degree of force that caused him to yelp. 'You're hurting me, Mum. Get off me.'

'What are you thinking? You'll hurt Harry.'

I held him in my arms for a second, before it happened. My small son burst into tears as if his heart was breaking.

'I want my Daddy back. Harry has got a Daddy and I want mine, too.'

Nothing prepares a parent for a moment like that. Greg turned off the television which was met with a tirade from the girls.

'We were watching that', announced Chloe.

'Tom always spoils everything. He's such a baby,' said Hannah.

I scooped my precious boy into my arms and took him into the dining room where we sat on the floor next to Susie's amazing Christmas tree. We cried in each other's arms next to tinsel and baubles that continued to shine, despite our misery.

'I want him too, Baby. I want him too.' I wiped snot from Tom's nose but let my own tears fall until I felt them wet around my neck. 'Sometimes life is very unfair Darling. We all miss Daddy.'

'Hannah doesn't. She said it's better without Daddy 'cos we go to bed later and sometimes we don't have to have a bath.' He nuzzled his wet face into mine. The door opened softly.

'Anything I can do?'

'I think we're coming back to watch the film in a minute Suz. Aren't we Tom?' He looked at me with pain in those pebble-brown eyes and I felt as inadequate as I ever had in my life. I had promised myself I'd never let my children know pain and, yet again, I'd failed them.

'We could play Buckaroo,' said Susie.

'Before we do anything you have to say sorry to Harry, don't you?'

'I will Mum.' He looked at me for a split-second before shooting off my lap. 'I'll bet I can play Buckaroo better than Hannah.' And he was gone, back into the thrill of Christmas as if nothing had happened.

'Are you OK? Let me get you a G&T

I was more shaken by Tom's distress than I let Susie see. The outburst had been a long time coming but I told myself it was healthy, that he'd let his anger out in the safety of family and friends.

'Think what life was like for you when you were five Katie. You're doing a really good job with them both, and they have all the care you never knew. You love them enough for two and that's the very best you can do. Come on. Buckaroo will work its magic on you too.' And it had. If only for a while.

Christmas had come and gone as it does every year. The Boxing Day walk was sensitively steered away from Cranham Woods; instead, we'd walked around the common close to Susie and Greg's home. The kids worried about the ponies huddled under a dry stone wall trying to thwart the wind. I was feeling less than merry, although the blast of fresh air was certainly beneficial after the food-stuffing I'd indulged in.

After Christmas I took a management job as Sister in Charge at a prestigious nursing home in the next village. Luckily, I'd found a dose of enthusiasm from somewhere and was at last happy to be using my training after five years away from the job market.

My negotiation with the Management Board resulted in a contract arranged around school times. (I guess there is some benefit to being a widow.) I was able to drop the children off in the mornings and be finished at three, in time to pick them up. I worked four days each week which gave me the luxury of a day to myself when the children were at school.

It felt like pastures new and progress along the path to recovery and survival.

Chapter 9

Kate had known in some distant recess of her mind that she was vulnerable when she met Jono Symonds, but she'd found it easy to ignore the nagging voice in her head. Tall, charming biker-boy Jono had masqueraded as the answer to every young widow's prayer. *It's too early for a new relationship but will a guy like Jono still be around when I'm ready. Probably not.*

Although she was still grieving for Chris and coming to terms with being a single mother, Kate hadn't considered the friendship to be harmful. It was kindness, wasn't it? What could possibly go wrong? But the friendship had been like warm chocolate melting over nuts; it had lots of bumps and irregularities but begged to be eaten.

Susie did say it was time to move on but I'm not sure she meant like this.

In the beginning, contact between them had been minimal but soon little things happened that brought them together. There was Jono's rescue-mission when Kate's car spluttered and died outside the school gates. It had offered up no more than a pathetic groan as she attempted to start it.

Kate avoided looking under the bonnet as she knew she'd get oil on her clothes. And anyway, she knew nothing about the workings of an engine. And Jono was the first person she'd thought of as she'd dug out his business card which she carried in her wallet. 'Just in case,' she'd told herself. A single woman can never have too many allies, can she?

She'd thrown herself on the mercy of the school secretary who had allowed her to use the office phone. Jono arrived within fifteen minutes.

It had been a simple matter of a loose connection on the battery and Kate had offered him coffee in her office as a thank you for spotting the problem which he had repaired in a few minutes. Then, a week or two later, he'd tinkered with her lawn mower which revved into life in his capable hands. He'd even mowed the lawn for her afterwards.

'Can't watch a beautiful lady mow a lawn, can I?'

'Charm doesn't work on me,' she'd told him.

'But it will. You'll see,' he'd smiled back. 'Before long Kate, you won't be able to live without me.'

She could have picked up a warning signal, but instead she'd observed him from the kitchen window as he'd walked behind the mower. His body was straight as a rod and graced with a rippling six-pack under manly, wide shoulders. *Bet he spends time in the gym. Even God didn't bless him with such perfection.* His glorious body sat under an intoxicating mop of hair that fell across his face when he moved. He'd looked so right in her garden. *Rather like a Greek God. I'll keep him under the rose bower, I think.*

Jono developed a habit of popping in to see her. Often, he happened to be passing her office around coffee time and left his black monster bike in the car park. Both he and his bike had given the care home residents a new talking point. He'd also called at Kate's house, but always parked his bike or car discreetly under the carport on those occasions. Sometimes he'd dropped in on the weekends but made every effort to avoid Kate's children.

There was a lot of eye contact and chemistry between them, and Kate's well-versed flirtation techniques were re-honed on

Jono. *He's got no chance*. He was partial to bacon sandwiches, no matter what the time of day, and bacon was now a constant on Kate's shopping list. Just in case. Chris had also loved bacon sandwiches and he often made them for a Sunday treat. They used to eat them in bed, usually after making love which always made him hungry. Jono also showed great appreciation for Kate's rich fruit cakes, preferably straight from the oven.

During one visit he'd browsed through her record and tape collection, and she'd discovered he was a Bruce Springsteen fan.

'I saw him in the States. He was up and coming back then but darned good. You obviously rate him.'

'Chris introduced me to his music. I love it.'

I wonder who he took to the concert. He's bound to have had girlfriends. Not that he ever talks about them. Perhaps I'll ask him. But not just yet.

Unfortunately, Jono wore Brut. It was the fragrance of the moment but also a scent that made him smell familiar. Kate had bought Brut for Chris as a stocking-filler for their last two Christmas's together and she'd caught a drift of it still clinging to his body when she'd identified him in the police morgue. Later, it was all she could remember about the gruelling task. He smelled as if he was still alive, but he wasn't, he was still warm, but dead. Now, there was something achingly familiar about the smell of Jono that suggested a rite of passage, an entitlement to his body. She'd wondered if he knew where his short visits were leading. *Of course he does. He's not stupid.*

Grieving for Chris was pushed aside as the old, headstrong Kate emerged like a butterfly with no innate sense of danger. She wanted Jono and so she took him.

Kate told Jono that she'd be working from home one Monday in April and invited him to have lunch with her. 'Nothing special but it would be nice, don't you think?' He'd offered to clear his diary for three hours and his eyes told her he was looking forward to it.

Kate had shopped at the local butchers to get the best quality pork chops which were scored and trimmed just the way she liked them. She found apple sauce in the freezer and bought a choice of delicious vegetables from Ron's veggie shop. Coffee ice-cream with a topping of Baileys was her favourite dessert. It was simple, but she hoped Jono would like it. As it turned out, they didn't have time for dessert.

Jono, surprisingly, was a bit of a chef. Not only did he prepare the vegetables, but he offered to grill the meat and make a mushroom sauce. Quite a man. Kate enjoyed the companionship of sharing the chores again. Having that feeling of a twosome was relaxing and she had few doubts where the afternoon would lead.

When she'd looked back on that lunch, she was never sure who had made the first move, but Jono had picked her up and laid her on the sofa where he'd taken her clothes off one item at a time. As each portion of bare flesh appeared he kissed it, as if paying homage to her body. She'd worried how the first sex in almost fifteen months would be. But she needn't have given it a thought as it felt like coming home. Home was the most fabulous, masculine body, and she claimed him for her own.

The passion that grew between them burned Kate deeply. A flame was ignited inside her each time they met, and it smouldered when they were apart. She now lay awake at night with Jono on her mind and the trauma of losing Chris undoubtedly diminished. She had eventually confided in Susie.

'I feel brand new. Re-born. That sounds bonkers, I know.'

'Too much God–Squad if you ask me. Or sneaky listening to the Stylistics.'

'Yeah right. Like you'd catch me doing either.'

'I'm not so sure. You sound in love to me.' Susie had looked serious. 'You're a big girl Kate, but vulnerable just now. Are you sure you've thought this through?'

'No. I've thought nothing through, but it's the first time I've felt safe since Chris died.'

Susie put an arm around her friend. 'Try to keep it in check. If you can. I can see the attraction, he's a good looking guy, but it would be easy to make a mistake, all things considered.'

'I feel like I'm getting a second chance to be happy.'

'How much do you know about him Kate?'

'I guess if he's good enough to courier for GCHQ then he must be squeaky-clean.

'Umm… Do you know if he's…

'I just enjoy being held Suz. Feeling wanted again. I know it's disgustingly soon after Chris, but it's kind of happened.'

Kate had known she couldn't excuse her behaviour, but she was infused with the man known as Jono Symonds. He was becoming an addiction.

She'd taken trips to Cheltenham and bought silk lingerie which she knew would drive him wild. She tried a new beauty salon that had just opened on the Promenade and had a pedicure and skin exfoliation. As Jono ripped every shred of clothes from her body, she wanted to be at her glowing best to keep his interest.

She found herself imagining him enveloped in her family. Tumbling with her kids; spending Christmas together. Writing cards and buying gifts for each other. Anything felt possible.

Their love making had been dynamic. He always left her in a slick of sweat and floating in sexual satisfaction. *He must have had a lot of women to know how to excite and satisfy like this. But who cares? It's the future that matters, not the past.*

Jono had entered Kate's life and turned it into a cyclone. He'd created a whirlwind of excitement and her physical need to be loved was met. But it should have been a red flag moment.

Chapter 10

Kate made a point of looking smart for work. *Jono might call by. Who knows?* She felt happiness bubbling near the surface and life was beginning to feel good again. Not many months ago she couldn't have imagined any kind of life ahead of her, and now she was starting to believe. And she had Jono to thank for that.

Jono said he might call into her office for coffee, so she'd chosen grey linen slacks and a white cotton shirt which she layered over a pale chocolate vest. Her brown, crocodile-skin ballet pumps were a favourite for work.

A new shampoo had Kate's tawny-red hair shining and it smelled divine. She'd caught it in a green velvet ribbon at the nape of her neck. Although she used little make up for work, she'd highlighted her eyes with a mid-green shimmer and tried her new lash-lengthening mascara. A touch of blusher and she'd been more than satisfied.

She'd taken turquoise parrot earrings from her jewellery box; it was the first time she'd worn them since Chris had given them to her the Christmas before he died. The mirror told her she looked decidedly jaunty.

Despite the efforts of her children to make her late for work, Kate managed to get there on time and was met with a cluster of jobs that needed her attention. The night nurse was ready to handover her patients and there was an undisclosed problem in the kitchen. Kate loved her job. Most aspects of running the nursing home had become her responsibility, as the owner was not a Registered nurse. Teresa, however, was a good employer who happily handed the reins to Kate. Both were lucky.

As Kate worked on the menus, she twiddled the turquoise parrots on her earlobes and pondered the short time Jono had been in her life. She felt safe around him and without doubt, he'd cut short her grieving for Chris.

When she considered their sex life, she could only describe it as electric. Jono's charisma rendered her helpless and his magic hands made her skin sing.

The bathroom mirror showed Kate that she'd developed a glow, and Susie remarked one day that she was looking 'pretty perky these days'. It was a much better look than 'grieving widow,' but guilt still had a nasty habit of kicking in at the slightest suggestion that she was over Chris. Only she knew that Chris would stay with her for the rest of her life.

The question over her children being properly introduced to Jono had been discussed a couple of times. They had been ultra-careful as Kate wasn't ready to involve them in her relationship yet, and Jono had shown little inclination to engage with Hannah and Tom. It meant that most of their time together was stolen during daylight hours when her house was empty.

Kate had no complaints, but she longed for the time they could all spend time together. Small niggles set in now and again about needing permanency or at least a sign of what the future held. Kate longed for more. She imagined them having a day at Bristol Zoo and looked forward to the time when they'd all enjoy a picnic or a bike ride together. Anything to make life feel normal. But their love was always this pulsing beast they kept in a box.

'I only want to protect the children, Kate. It isn't personal. Doesn't it feel rather early days for too much mingling? I don't want them hurt.'

Kate said she understood his caution but constantly pondered it. It was like a nagging toothache refusing to be ignored.

Chapter 11

Kate's relationship with Jono began to run at a scary pace. Suddenly she understood why Chris had never quite been enough for her. She decided this time she was truly in love. Jono left her gasping for breath and gave her sleepless nights when she lay in her bed without him. Always longing for his touch, she could think of little else when they were apart.

Little by little he'd made himself indispensable. He'd romanced her in a way no one ever had, and she'd been putty in his hands. He never asked about her past and he never mentioned a future. They'd fucked for the moment and to hell with anything else.

After a few months of their high-octane romance, Kate began to wonder if it was time to let Jono meet the children. Her initial fears were blanked by a belief that Jono was all she'd ever need. *I'd never sleep around if we were married. Or even if we weren't. He truly is enough for me. More than enough.*

Jono convinced her it was still too early for him to meet the children properly and she convinced herself she loved his caution. *He's even good father material. How lucky can I get?* However, Kate hoped that Jono would soon instigate a permanence to their relationship. They'd been spending more and more daytime hours together and she longed to have him in her bed at night.

Eventually, Kate decided to ask Jono if they had a future together. She'd lost sleep over how to broach the subject but felt it was time to take the initiative. *Why are you so impulsive? Can't you enjoy this for what it is? No. No I can't.* She was beginning to feel like his 'bit on the side', although she'd told herself that was ridiculous. And so, in a rare, weak moment she had asked him.

'Jono...I...I'm not too sure how to say this. or even if I should but...I want more. *Now you sound like bloody Oliver Twist.* 'More from our relationship, that is, more than it is now. Isn't it time we went public?'

He'd caressed her hair and looked into her eyes. 'Well, you are a keen little bunny, aren't you? If I didn't know better, I'd think you were in love with me.'

Kate blushed. 'Could be I am. Would you mind?'

Jono had passed the moment off with humour, but an exact answer wasn't forthcoming. Kate felt stupid and guilty and could have bitten her tongue off the moment the words tumbled out. They'd been lying in an after-glow of sexual pleasure and she, sure as hell, had dampened the mood.

No answer had been forthcoming and as the week progressed, Kate imagined there was a shadow of distance between them. She'd been unable to define it, but it felt as if something wasn't right. *Maybe I'm more invested in the relationship than Jono. And maybe I've pushed him away. Serve you right if he scarpers. He probably thinks you're a needy cow.* But he had phoned her at work a couple of days later.

'Can you talk?'

'Sure.'

'Can I come round?'

'Of course you can. The boss is away. What's up? You sound serious.'

'You asked a question on Tuesday. A very important one.'

'I did'. Kate gulped and licked her dry lips. She passed her fingers through her hair and tucked stray curls behind her ears.

'I want to come and see you. To give my answer. It's all I've thought about, ever since you asked me.'

Kate had hung up the phone and had a quick tidy around her office. Jono arrived in less than ten minutes, dressed in his killer black leathers and with an unusually watered-down smile. Kate had a feeling she wasn't going to like his answer, even before he spoke. He kissed her. *That feels the same.* She'd placed the 'busy' sign outside her office door and closed it. Jono sat in the visitor's chair while Kate dragged her office chair to sit beside him. Her mouth felt like the sandbox her kids used to play in, and she noticed a tremble in her hands.

'Let's have coffee.' She bounced up to fill the kettle and busied herself with the mugs. *Why do I feel that life is never going to be the same in about two short minutes?* 'And so,' she ventured, 'what is it to be? Will I wilt like a limp lettuce when I hear the answer, or drag your clothes from your body?'

'Probably neither…promise you won't hate me?'

'I'm not sure I can make that promise with no information.' Kate's heart rate had risen to a dull beat in her ears. 'Probably best if you spit it out.' She paused and looked at him, but he didn't meet her eyes.

'I can't do it Kate. I'm so sorry...I'm...the problem is...I'm married... and I have two children.'

'You bastard.' Blood flushed her face. 'You lying, cheating bastard.' As Kate turned on him, she'd accidentally thrown scalding coffee all over her chocolate-brown, leather pumps. 'All this time and... *you're bloody married'*.

She'd walked to the window and stared at the carpark, trying to calm the flush she could feel creeping up her neck. *Never a good look.* She'd brushed her wet eyes with the back of her shaking hand and wondered if she'd smudged her mascara. *Oh no you don't. Don't you dare cry*.

'Why did you do it?' She rounded on him with fury. 'Did it give you a kick to pick up a grieving widow and *'keep her happy'* for a while?' Kate knew her temper was getting out of control, but she didn't care. 'What an easy touch I was, eh? Promiscuous Kate rides again. Only this time I didn't know you were a married man, did I?'

'I've fallen in love with you Kate. It's as simple as that.'

'That speaks volumes about your marriage, Jono. But it isn't simple, is it?'

'I'll sort it, Kate. Trust me. Have a little faith, can't you?'

'Faith? I should have faith in a cheating liar, should I? How does that work?' She'd pushed her chair back where it belonged and sat down with a distance between them. 'So how are you intending to clear up this mess? Bump her off?'

Jono moved to touch her, but Kate shoved him hard with the palm of her hand.

'And we'll be together. I promise.' He'd caught Kate's arm and held her. 'Just give me time and I'll leave her.'

Kate snatched her arm away from him. 'Does she have a name? This wife?'

'Emma. She's called Emma.'

Kate couldn't form the word. *It doesn't matter what she's called. He still has a wife.*

'Well get out of my office and go home to *Emma*. Would she want you if she knew about me?

Jono had looked at Kate with an expression she couldn't read. 'We will be together Kate. Just you wait and see. I'll fix this.'

'Bugger off Jono. You have no idea what you've done. It's over.'

He'd left quietly. Kate struggled to get her head back into work-mode and made another coffee while the kettle was hot. She'd contemplated her stupidity. *Why would such a dishy bloke be available? Anyone with half a brain would have suspected he was married.*

And that was it.

Kate shuffled some paperwork across her desk. She couldn't grasp the enormity of what he'd done to her. He'd shredded her emotions and dashed her dreams.

As she'd sipped her coffee she could feel her temper cooling. She told herself she should have kept the relationship in check. Instead, she'd fallen in love only to find all the emotions she'd invested in him were built on fallow ground. There was no foundation to anything he'd said or done. He was a man of straw. And, to compound the issue, Chris and Jono's faces had become inter-changeable of late. When she and Jono had made love, it was no longer clear whose bed she was in. That was a burden too far and she had only herself to blame.

Chapter 12

That evening, after the children were in bed, Jono rang her doorbell. There he stood like a marble God, with a bottle of wine in his hand and a smile to melt the icecaps.

'Please let me in Kate. Please.' He'd edged inside and any sense of self-preservation was lost to Kate. He'd kissed her hair.

'Mmm, you always smell delicious.'

'What do you want, Jono? There's nothing to say.'

'But you're wrong Katie. We'll be happy when I've left Emma.

'You won't leave home and it's cruel to say you will. Why don't you make a clean break and bugger off?'

He'd sprung across the carpet and wrapped his arms around her. He'd nuzzled her hair and slid a hand inside her blouse. He found her mouth and kissed her hard. Almost too hard, making Kate wince.

'Stop. Stop this, Jono. It's over. I've told you.'

'It'll never be over Kate. I *will* have you.' And he'd picked her up and carried her into the kitchen where he'd taken her on the breakfast bar. He'd entered her as if he owned her and left her feeling dirty. Why had she allowed him to do that? Where was her sense of dignity?

Tears flowed. She'd become spellbound by Jono Symonds and could see no antidote. *Does he mean it? Should I give him time to sort out his marriage? Don't be a stupid cow. He's fooling you and you're falling for it.*

He sat himself on the sofa and she watched him sink into the cushions. *I'm such a fool. Make him leave. Get him out.*

'You need a cuddle, Kate. He patted the sofa beside himself and moved a cushion to make a space for her. She'd done as he asked. 'Let me calm you. I want to hold you.' Jono had looked into her tearful face. 'Why do you doubt me, Kate? It's very hurtful you know.'

'How can I not? You are a cheat and a liar and that doesn't equate to love in my book. And don't you turn this on me.' Kate felt her colour rising.

'I've been hurt too. I'm not made of stone.'

'But you're the one responsible for this mess. Why did you let it happen when you knew you weren't free? Do you make a habit of it? I suppose I'm one in a long line of conquests.'

He had no answers.

'I'll leave her Kate. The marriage was over yonks ago.'

'No, you won't, Jono. You'll never leave the children.'

'Anything, I'll do anything to keep you. You see if I don't.'

Kate had grabbed a box of tissues from the coffee table and dabbed the damage to her face. Her auburn curls were wet and she snagged them behind her ears.

'I love you. I bloody well love you.' In a weak moment she'd spilled her heart onto the warmth of his chest. Deep sobs exploded. 'But you're a mirage. Nothing I believed about you is true. How dare you fool me into loving you when you knew I was vulnerable.

He'd held her and they'd cried in each other's arms.

'Don't Kate. Don't. He'd wrapped himself around her and coaxed her body to stillness.

'I suppose I've always known there's a pecking order in your life,' Kate conceded. 'But I didn't know what it was. It's my own fault.' She'd beaten his arm with her fist. 'You're married and I should have read the signs.'

He'd handed her his hanky. 'Don't Kate. I love you and it breaks my heart to see what I've done. But we will be together. Believe me.'

Kate had blown her nose with the force of a rhino and thrown his hanky on the arm of the sofa.

'I blame myself. But we will be together. You can push me away for the moment, but I'll make it happen.'

Kate was the first to break the moment. She moved his arm from her body and dragged herself from his warmth, noting the little boy rather than the married father of two on her sofa.

As he'd left her house that night, he cupped her face in his hands and kissed her. The touch of his baby-soft mouth drained blood from her knees while his eyes had scrutinised her with heart-stopping familiarity. *But he's a bastard, so get used to life without him.*

The gentle closing of the door behind him stamped finality on life as she knew it. Kate filled the kettle and shook coffee beans into the grinder. Absent-mindedly, she spray wiped all trace of Jono Symonds from the breakfast bar and placed two mugs next to the coffeepot. She'd pulled a packet of chocolate biscuits from the shelf, opened it, and crammed her mouth with calories.

She could still feel his touch. Sensed his breath on her neck. Her brain was addled by a devastation she'd known before, although familiarity with grief gave no benefit second time around. *He's a shit. Remember that. He let you love him, but he's married.*

She'd showered, crawled into her pyjamas, snagged her hair into a scrunchie, scrubbed her teeth, then lain in the darkness thinking about him. The firmness of his body, the energy, the gentleness, the shuddering orgasms and the love he'd poured into her life, now had a red alert warning on them.

She checked her fatherless children, deep in their dreamless slumber. One a waft of pink nightie in her bunk bed and the other one snuggled under his Superman duvet. A scent of bath-time lingered and made her smile, despite her misery. Is there anything nicer than small children fresh from the bath, glowing and pink and bathed in the fragrance of shampoo?

The children had been the one thing that had dragged Kate through the loss of Chris, almost two years before. She had been a widow before she turned thirty and still noted the pitying eyes of those who crossed the road rather than speak to her. She'd learned to deal with tearful nights and fretting children. Life had dumped on her, but not for the first time. She'd been all too familiar with pain, but this time it was of her own making. *Thank goodness I hadn't let him into the children's lives. At least that's a positive to hang on to.*

She couldn't sleep. Inevitably, reflection on the past months crowded her brain and she'd been shocked at her lack of self-preservation around Jono. Falling so quickly wasn't really her style. But she'd let Jono slip into her life as stealthily as the silk undies he'd loved to glide down her body. It had only taken months to allow Jono to inveigle her heart, rather than the year it had taken her to become invested in Chris. Jono had melted her resolve in a way Chris had never done.

She'd miss him more than she could measure. Sometimes he'd brought her a fillet steak to ensure she ate properly. 'Kids leftovers for tea aren't good enough, young lady,' he'd told her when he caught her nibbling a fish finger. 'I want to know you're keeping your strength up. Just for me.'

Sometimes she'd found a box of chocolates he'd smuggled into her bedroom with an 'I love you' note on the bedside table. He'd take her bin out, send flowers when it wasn't her birthday and the thing she'd miss most, he'd made her body dance in a way she'd never experienced before.

Eventually she'd seen the dawn breaking through a chink in the curtains and the full force of last night's drama rose with the ferocity of floodwater. She'd dozed intermittently but had to get the kids to school, and she had no idea where she would find the energy. She'd made mental lists; homework, reading books and clean uniforms. But she could still hear the roar of Jono's motorbike ringing in her ears. Now she would have to find a new normality in her life, and it broke her heart.

When the alarm eventually dragged Kate from her bed, she'd felt a wobble in her knees and a thickness in her head, both more deserved after a night on the booze. This was the second time she'd loved and lost, and experience had taught her she was heading for a long haul of abject misery. She had never handled rejection well, and losing someone you love was no easier second time around. If anything, the finality of death was an easier concept to grasp. Easier than the shifting sands that had pulled Jono from under her feet.

But Kate had a well-defined, common-sense-gene and it was quick to kick-in within twenty four hours. Jono had gone. *And good riddance*. She knew she could mow the lawn and the garage always serviced her car before he came along. Who needs gifts of perfume anyway? She would manage. She didn't need Jono Symonds. *Who are you kidding Kate? He's as addictive as heroin.*

As the days went by, she couldn't find the courage to tell Susie that Jono was married. She would, of course, but not until she had to. She would scrub the bastard from her phone book. That was a positive step, wasn't it? It's always better not to leave temptation in the way, she'd decided. Like a cream cake or too much red wine. That's it; she'd treat him like alcohol addiction. She thought the AA had something called a ten-step plan and she'd conceive her own pathway to get over Jono Symonds.

Chapter 13

After the truth broke Kate's life apart, it only took Jono Symonds five days before he'd met her from work. He looked as miserable as Kate felt when he'd parked at the nursing home, although Kate didn't notice him at first. She was unlocking her car when he stood behind her.

'Jono. You frightened the life out of me.'

'I had to see you. I know you want a clean break, but I can't face life without you.

'Try harder.'

'Are you managing Kate? Without me?'

'Why would I need you in my life? I can do anything on my own. I'm used to it.'

'You sound hard.' What have I done to you?'

'Yes, I'm hard. Think of me as a cheap screw. A girl who did it for money, maybe.' Kate's face flared. 'It's tough for me too, but the mess is yours, not mine.'

'I know and I'm sorry.'

'Sorry isn't good enough. I've wanted to ring you,' Kate spat at him. But I didn't. You can't have it all Jono. Nobody has it all.'

'I know. I'm sorry I came. It was unfair.'

'Yes, it bloody well was. I'm heart-broken Jono Symonds. That's twice in ten years that I've loved someone and twice I've been left with nothing.'

Jono took a step towards her and offered an arm for comfort. Suddenly the sluice gate opened. Unchecked emotion flowed. The hurt that she'd tried so hard to hold back, gushed like a leaking pipe. Kate sobbed. Standing in the carpark, leaning on her car, she was beyond words.

Jono wrapped his arms around her and she allowed him to guide her to the passenger seat of his own car.

'I can't bear this Kate. I love you but I've hurt you so deeply.'

'I'll get by. I always manage on my own. I've got the children and that's enough for me.'

'You don't mean it Kate. You should never be alone. You deserve better than this.'

'Damn right I do.'

Jono had reached into the back seat and retrieved a box of tissues. Kate blew her nose and attempted to pull herself together.

'I know you don't believe me, but I will leave her. I will have you.

'I'm not asking you to do that. How can I, after the childhood I've had? Go away and at least be a good father.'

'I'm going to be with you Kate. I don't care what consequences there are. We'll be together. It will just take time.'

'I've got to fetch the kids. Just look at me. I'm a mess.' Kate pulled the sun-visor down to inspect her mottled face in the mirror and a photo of a dark haired woman, two kids and unmistakably Jono, dropped into her lap. Jono took it from her and placed it in the glove compartment.

'You look good to me.' He gazed at her teary face.

'But I'm not the most important person in your life. Apparently.'

Jono had looked away. 'If only you knew Kate. Why don't I take you to pick up Tom and Hannah and then I'll bring you back to your car. I don't think you should drive in this state Kate.'

Kate looked at her watch. 'It's three fifteen. They'll be out in fifteen minutes.' She knew taking his offer made sense, but her head was arguing with her heart.

'OK. But we'll have to go right now.'

They'd driven in custard-thick silence. Kate kept her eyes on the road, her heart was pumping blood into her ears. Thump, thump. She was sure he must hear it. *So, she's dark haired and pretty.*

The children were coming out of class as they arrived.

'Stay here. I'll collect them.' Kate forced a smile and told the children they were going in a friend's car to the nursing home.

'Why?' asked Hannah. Why aren't you in your own car Mum?'

'You ask too many questions young lady. Remember Jono? He's giving us a lift.'

'Hi guys. Had a good day at school?' Jono had leaned against the bonnet of his car looking like a film star.

'Why do adults always ask the same question?' stropped Hannah.

Wish you'd brought your motorbike. I could have had a proper ride,' Tom gushed.

'Over my dead body.'

'I don't know what your problem is,' said Tom as he hopped into the back seat of Jono's car. 'Come on Miss Fussy Boots. Get in. Jono, you're a real cool dude!'

Kate smiled despite her misery. 'God knows what she'll be like when she's a teenager.' She checked their seat belts were in place.

'She'll probably sail through unscathed, Jono laughed.

'Umm. Maybe not. Why should I be that lucky?'

'Shall we stop for ice cream? My treat, asked Jono.'

'Yes please,' came from the back seat.

Kate was furious. Now she'd look the bad guy when she said no. 'Not today. Wait until the weekend for treats.'

'Mum. You never let us have treats.'

'See what you've done,' she seethed at Jono.

'Sorry. I didn't think.'

'Not your strong point, I'll give you that.'

At the nursing home carpark Kate made a quick exit to get the whingeing kids into her car. Jono had watched her leave, but she didn't look back.

'It's rude not to say thank you. You always tell us that.'

'Sometimes, just sometimes you could cut me some slack, Hannah.'

When Kate got the children to bed that evening, she'd rung Susie and broken the news about Jono. 'I feel such a bloody fool and...and I love him Suz. I really love the bastard.'

'I'll come round. Greg's watching some boring documentary and I'd welcome the break.'

The sorry tale came tumbling out as they opened a bottle of Merlot.

'And you never picked up a clue? He never dropped the smallest hint?'

'If only. I can't believe I've been sucked in like a sixteen year old. How many times have I been round the block?'

'The trouble is you're vulnerable and the snide bugger went for the jugular. I've a good mind to door-knock his wife.'

'I've already thought about that, but it wouldn't help. I still can't have him, can I?'

'No, but sisters should stick together. She needs to know what he's done.'

'Well, I'm not going to do that, and I'll get on with my life without him. Although right now I have no idea how I'll do it.'

'You will. You're the strongest woman I know. And I can lend you Greg if life gets too tough.'

'Ha ha, he'd run a mile if I so much as flirted with him. And you - you'd have my guts for garters. No. There surely is a way forward but it's not with your man. Kind as the offer is.'

'Well, you know we're both there for you. However much of a scrape you get into.'

After they'd polished off the bottle, Kate wished Susie goodnight and cleared the glasses. She braced herself for another sleepless night. The doors were secured and both children checked. Tom had thrown half his duvet to the floor, so she covered him and kissed his forehead. She showered and fell into bed. As she'd watched the clock wind down the hours, she could think only of Jono. Sexy, perfect Jono.

The next day Kate staggered into work feeling like chewed up string. 'Good morning, Heidi.'

'Morning Sister.' Heidi the cleaner was always first in and good for a brew at any time, regardless of her duties. 'Looks like you could do with a nice cup of tea. Late night, was it?'

'Something like that. Tea would be great. Thanks.' Kate let herself into her office and sorted the post before checking on her patients.

'Ruby looks frail this morning.' Heidi leaned on the door jamb and, as ever, she was up for a natter. She was better than a detective. 'I had to call night nurse when I got in. She was half out of bed, and I had to hold on to her to stop her falling.'

'Thank you, Heidi. Well spotted. I'll get the change-over report in five minutes. Could you be sure you've filled up the paper towels please.'

Heidi had sauntered off, humming a tune of dubious origin.

Later in the morning Kate realised with a shock that her period was late. She was as regular as clockwork but due to all the upset, she hadn't noticed her dates.

She'd slipped out to buy a testing kit and then took two hours to find the courage to use it. And it wasn't good news. Well, not good news for a widow with two children and a defunct relationship. *This is one disaster too far.*

Chapter 14

After a traumatic day and the discovery that she was pregnant, Kate needed to shop for food and then, after a hasty tea, it was cubs for Tom and supervised homework for Hannah. It was nearly eight o'clock before she got the children to bed and found time to grasp the new reality; she was adding another child to the family.

She picked up a pile of unopened mail before settling on the sofa for a couple of hours of peace. There was the usual array of junk mail, a letter from her pal in America who hoped she was getting her life back on track, and a letter which popped out of an expensive, embossed envelope. The content caused her to frown. "Sometimes we make wrong decisions in life. You'd better put your mistake right or there will be consequences." Kate had no idea what it could mean. The sender was unidentified.

A cold shiver ran up her arm. *What the hell is this? Someone's idea of a joke?* She rang Susie. 'Hi Suz. Sorry to ring so late. I may have a problem. Is Greg about?

'He loves a damsel in distress. Hang on. I'll get him.

'Kate. I can't remember when you last needed me; probably, when you couldn't get rid of that widow-chaser at the PTA meeting last year. What can I do for you? I'll rephrase that, what can I do for you that my wife wouldn't object to?'

'I heard that!' Susie could be heard laughing at her husband's inane joke.

'Hi Greg. I'm probably worrying over nothing, but I've had a weird letter. Can I read it to you and see what you think?'

'Sure honeybun. Go for it.'

Kate read the letter to Greg. 'It makes no sense. I've made a mental list of patients and their families. I've tried to think if I've had a disagreement in the past week or two. Nothing springs to mind. I did refuse a place in the nursing home to a dementia patient last week. The family were pissed off, but they must be desperate to try blackmail.'

'You've not been having clandestine dates, have you?'

'No. This is a bit of a mystery. Do you think it's got a slightly threatening ring to it?

'Hmm. It is a bit odd, but I don't think you need to worry. Have a G&T and an early night.

But Kate wasn't able to get comfy. She'd plumped pillows, read awhile and finally opened her bedroom window in the hope that fresh air would help her drift off. She'd made a quick check on the kids and then lain in the dark with her thoughts.

I need this like a hole in the head. If I tell Susie I'm carrying Jono's child, she'll scoot me off to the clinic quicker than I can down a glass of red. But do I really want another child? Now that I don't have Jono, it's a big consideration. And what will I tell the kids? 'Mummy was sleeping with Jono, but he turned out to have another family, so now that I'm pregnant we shall all have to look after each other.' Yeh right.

Kate had woken at five with a feeling that something was wrong, but it took her a minute to remember what. The baby? No, the letter. Who the hell would send something like that? She pondered the problems as first-light cast a shard on her duvet. A light breeze caressed the cords of a puppet the kids had made her which lived on her bedroom wall. It mimicked yacht-lines singing along the harbour wall in Scilly.

For a moment she'd let her mind wander. She and Chris had enjoyed magical holidays on the islands with the children who had loved their bucket and spade jaunts. As she lay in a crumpled heap of bedding it was easy to recall the BBQ's on deserted beaches, coming home by small boat and watching the phosphorescence glow on the water. All had been unforgettable experiences. *Yeh, yeh. All in the past. You have to move on Kate Roseland.*

The need to address the baby issue wouldn't go away. *It needs care and thought and shouldn't be hurried*, was her first decision. Or was that an excuse? Was she procrastinating? Did she just need to get on with a plan?

Kate decided to tell Susie about her pregnancy, if only to share the load. She rang and invited her to coffee.

'It sounded serious on the phone,' Susie said. 'What's up?'

'In a way it is serious.' And so, Kate told her.

'Why are we even discussing this? You know the right thing to do, don't you?

'I do, but this is a life we're talking about. A little person. How can I discard it like an unwanted sack of rubbish?

'No. No, stop right there,' Susie's arms rotated like windmills. 'This is a blob of jelly that is so unformed it could be a maggot. You're only five weeks max and this nonsense has got to stop. Anyway, if you had it, how would you manage? Would Chris have condoned another mouth to feed? On your own? Don't forget that bit Katie. You're a single mother.'

'Using Chris is below the belt, and you know it.'

'I'm sorry. It was a shitty thing to say. But I feel so angry. I'm angry with Jono for all his deceit; angry with you and angry with myself 'cos I'm not any help.'

'But you are. Just to talk about it is a relief. I couldn't believe the test.'

'Listen to me. You're not a quitter and we'll sort this together.'

'I can't see any way out of this. What if I get rid of it but can't live with the guilt?'

'Isn't guilt better than years of drudgery? It wouldn't be easy with three kids. How could you work?' Susie flicked her blond hair out of her eyes. 'This is what we're going to do. You wait a week and during that time make a list of all the pros and cons. Meanwhile I'll try to be more impartial. Sound like a plan?'

As always, Susie had dug out the relevant facts and ditched the dross.

A week later the decision was no easier. Kate still struggled with washing a little being down the pan. But how could she support Tom and Hannah if she had a baby to look after? That would be one step too far, even for the willing Poppy. Kate had to accept that it was likely she'd go ahead with a termination.

She and Susie discussed it late one evening and Kate decided she would at least make an appointment with her doctor. He confirmed she was about seven weeks pregnant, and the clinic appointment was made. Susie said she would be there for her.

Kate had little time to think about the letter or the upcoming procedure. The children needed fancy dress for Halloween and there was the usual fight brewing about firework night. In the Roseland household fireworks were a no-go area.

'If you'd nursed as many children as I have who've been burnt by fireworks, then you'd know why I'm 'being so mean.'

'It's not fair. You never let us have fireworks. Tess's mother lets her...blah blah blah'. It was the same every year.

After a busy day at work and having survived the firework debacle, Kate had put her feet up and tuned into her favourite television drama. And she'd suddenly missed Chris with heart-wrenching sadness. They'd always watched the programme together, and usually an argument arose about how it might end. But they always cuddled on the sofa. A loneliness, kept at bay of late, suddenly hit her like a blow to the gut.

The doorbell rang just as she'd settled down with a cup of coffee. Kate cursed. It was her first minute of peace all day. If she'd listened to Chris when he'd tried to instruct her how to record programmes, she'd have known how to use the up-to-the-minute machine, bought just before he died. But she didn't, so she'd turned the volume down and went to answer the door.

He stood there, looking fabulous in his black leathers which caused Kate to take a deep breath, although no words formed.

Jono walked past her and into the sitting room as if he had a rite of passage to her domain.

'I love this too,' he'd said, glancing at the television. 'I'll bet the uncle did it.'

'What the hell do you think you're playing at? You've got a nerve, barging in here.'

He had placed a finger on her lips. 'Sssh. Although I love you when you're angry, I love you best with no clothes on.'

'Get out. We've got nothing left to say to each other.'

'What I have in mind doesn't need words.'

And so, he'd sweet talked her into having sex and she melted under his touch. And it was oh so good; any man who peels off black leathers with an erect penis means business. He had always been able to bring her to orgasm, and this time was no exception. He was an unselfish lover who could delight her in ways she'd never experienced.

When it was over, she'd placed bacon under the grill while Jono made coffee. She hadn't notice him pick up her clinic appointment letter from the work surface. The next instant she'd felt a swift blow to the side of her head. She'd staggered to hold onto the sink which she clung to as if her life depended on it.

'You little tart. So, you think you can scrape my baby into a hospital waste-bin, do you? You've got a lot to learn about me, sweetheart.'

'Jono. You hit me.' Kate held her head which was zinging from the blow.

'Nothing gets past you, does it?'

Kate felt dizzy and angry. She sat on a stool and watched the bacon burn.

'I'll deal with that, shall I?' Jono proceeded to make two sandwiches, brown sauce included and sat opposite her while he munched. 'Not hungry?'

Kate felt a dribble of blood run down her forehead.

'Oh darling. Let me deal with that. Do you often have falls? You need to tell your doctor. Falls can be indicative of other things, you know.'

Kate pushed his hand away. She couldn't focus; her head was spinning, and her body was a shaking mess.

'Get out. Leave me alone. I've told you it's over. Accept it.'

'But I told you I'd leave her. I also told you you'll never be free of me. We're meant to be together.'

'Get out before I ring the police.'

'How are the children? I think I'll pop upstairs and see if they're OK.'

Kate found legs to reach the doorway. 'Over my dead body you go anywhere near my children.'

'But you're not so protective of my baby, are you? It's OK to slide that one down the sink.'

'It's not your decision Jono. I'm the one who will have to raise this baby. I'm a single mother, in case you've forgotten. And the baby has a thug for a father, it would appear.

'I'll move in. We'll get married Kate. Divorce is easy these days.' He'd stroked her face which bloomed with a purple bruise. 'You are so impatient. You're headstrong Kate. You need to know I always get what I want.' He'd placed an arm around her and stroked her hair. 'God, I love your hair.

I'd really like you to leave.' Kate sounded cooler than she felt. She'd looked at the congealed bacon sandwich and felt sick.

'I'm not going anywhere until you promise to keep our baby. It's ours Kate. Born of love.'

This is like some bloody two a penny romance. Her face was beginning to throb. 'OK. OK Jono, I won't go to the clinic. Now will you go.

Chapter 15

Kate

I tried to hide from Susie at the school gate, but she bounded over like an Easter Bunny to ask how I was.

'Heavens, Kate. What's happened to you?'

'I...the kids were playing hide and seek, and they slammed the door in my face.'

'You need to do better than that Katie. Tell me what happened.'

'I'm late for work. We'll talk later.'

'Now. I need you to tell me right now.'

I knew Susie wouldn't give up until I told her the grim details, so we chatted in her car.

'Not only shouldn't he have been at the house, but he hit you. Is that the first time he's touched you Kate?'

'It is. Honestly. It is. I'd tell you if he'd done it before.'

'What provoked him? Did you have a row?'

'He saw the clinic appointment letter. He's furious.'

'Not as furious as I am. How dare he?'

I saw colour rise in her cheeks.

'Suz I've got to go. I'm already late for work. Pop in for coffee if you can. I'm in the office all day.'

When Susie called for an afternoon cup of tea, she was still furious. 'You seem pretty cool about it.'

'I'm not. But what can I do? He's never shown a temper before, but I suppose it is his baby, too.'

'Listen to me.' I was listening.

'That lying sod has no rights to your baby. He's proved he's not father material and he's married as well. What more do you need?'

'Hey, don't shout. I've decided to go ahead with the termination. If anything, I'm more determined than ever. But I'm afraid about what he'll do when he finds out.'

'You need to take Greg's advice. Go to the police.'

'Mmm…I could, but I want to see if this is the end of it. Perhaps, if he thinks there is no baby, he'll leave me alone.'

'Pigs might fly. Why don't you alter the time of the appointment in case he decides to tip up?'

'That's a good idea. I'll give them a ring now.' Susie left to pick up a prescription while I made the call.

I took time to contemplate.

I realise I'm struggling to get a handle on my life and the pregnancy on top of Jono's antics has left me anxious. It's a mess, no, to be brutally honest, it's a catastrophe. A little life is growing inside me with disregard for the kind of parents it will inherit. What use are an inadequate mother and an absent, violent father? How can I bring up another child? I'm not sure I'm a fit mother to the two I have.

I wasn't well carrying Hannah or Tom. Morning sickness dogged me for months and I was lucky I didn't have to drag myself out of bed each morning to go to work. Chris was a hero. He stayed home with me on the worst days. And when I had a demanding, fifteen month old Humpy to contend with, he often took charge. I spent hours vomiting and sleeping. This time, I know I will be on my own.

I try not to waste head space on Jono, and he doesn't make contact for the next forty eight hours. I am gradually seeing him in a different light. He is the inordinate conman. A womaniser. He is everything I don't need in my life. What had I been thinking? How was I so stupid? *You wanted him to be a knight in shining armour. You wanted rescuing and only saw what he allowed you to see.*

I knew he'd never leave his wife and children, and he appeared to be incapable of facing up to his own lies or acknowledging the damage he's done. He has this mantra, 'we will be together' which, to be honest, is starting to feel a bit creepy.

I've dabbled with married men before but this time it's different. Firstly, I didn't know Jono was married, and unfortunately, I love him. But something doesn't feel right about encouraging him to leave his children. I have no qualms about stealing him from his wife, she's old enough to look after her man, and if she can't then she deserves everything she gets. But not the children. Why should they grow up without their father, because of me?

I can move on without Jono. I know I can do this. I'm good at starting over and I have the determination to make a clean break. But I have no idea how to stop Jono pestering me. He behaves as if nothing has changed. And now I suppose, he'll keep asking about the baby. It's as if he can't grasp the fact that he can't have it all. I can move forward, but only if I get him out of my life. I can pick up the pieces, one fragment at a time, but my ability to cope appears to make him angry.

Jono regularly phones me in the evenings. When I answer he starts the conversation as if nothing has happened; it's as if I haven't told him it's over. And then he pleads with me. He reminds me how great our sex-life was, *as if I need any reminder*. And then the nastiness begins. He tells me I'm nothing without him and that wretched phrase, 'we will be together' keeps coming at me until I want to scream. Often, I hang up, but he rings again and again. I take the phone off the hook, but he reports a fault to the telephone company, and they test my line with a loud screech to inform me my phone is off the hook. It feels as if I can't win. I worry about my kids who are always upstairs, safe in their dreams, and I worry that they'll wake and hear something they shouldn't.

Sometimes Jono parks in the nursing home carpark when I'm due to leave work. He doesn't acknowledge me; he simply watches. Greg and Susie have warned me that he's become a stalker. I think they're right and it's creepy. He seems to have a personality defect that I never noticed before and I can't be sure which Jono is around. The kind, loving man who romanced me or the demanding, angry, unreasonable Jono who hit me and makes the nuisance phone calls. It's getting tedious and scary too.

The appointment is looming. I can think of nothing else. Luckily, the kids appear blissfully unaware of my stress. Tom occasionally mentions 'that nice man with the motorbike,' but Jono isn't on Hannah's radar, thank goodness.

I don't know if it's my nurse training that gives me strong views about terminating a life, or the knowledge that I was unwanted and I, too, could have been flushed down the loo. I'm not Catholic and I've not taken any other leap of faith that's likely to indoctrinate my views, but I can't help fretting that it's not right to kill a baby before it has a chance to draw breath. I guess my moral compass touches base with decency at some point and thank goodness for that. What if my birthmother had got rid of me in a shower of blood because she didn't want me? But there is no question of following in her footsteps and having my baby adopted. The biggest problem I'm wrestling with is that I know I'll love it the moment it pops out, even if it is Jono's. But the alternative keeps me awake at night, too. How could I have been so stupid? *Did I secretly long to have Jono's baby and live happily ever after? I wouldn't be the first silly cow to go down that path. But I didn't know he was married, did I?*

I've promised Susie I'll make a final decision by tomorrow. I guess it will go the way of common sense, but it's a tough call. The appointment letter stares me down from the kitchen corkboard.

The school run calls and interrupts my misery. Collecting the children always perk me up and I have left myself just twenty minutes to get them. I'm picking Susie's two up today and bringing them home for tea.

After an exhausting couple of hours with four hungry children, Greg picks up Harry and Chloe. I put mine to bed and read them stories which always has a calming effect on all three of us. Tom tells me about his activities at school while Hannah tells me nothing. Zilch. It's like pulling teeth to get any information from her.

I want a glass of red wine, but I can't have it. This baby deserves that much respect. The termination will happen soon enough. Is that thought supposed to induce sleep? No chance.

It's eight thirty and already dark. And I still want a glass of red wine. I go to the kitchen to make a brew and as I'm waiting for the kettle to boil, I think I catch sight of a shadow passing the window. I jump and almost scream. My back garden is an enclosed space so who the hell could be out there at this time of night? Something moved again from the back door and across the patio. My heart is thumping like a printing press. I can't find the courage to open the back door or put the outside light on. Who could it be? *Shit, maybe it's a burglar casing the joint.*

Just as the kettle boils, I see it again. This time I scream. It's an involuntary noise from the back of my throat. There's a man in a black balaclava moving belly-down across the lawn like a terrorist. I check the door lock and race to secure the front door and the conservatory, too. I reach for the phone and dial 999 and try to calm myself so that I can tell the operator what is happening.

'Are you alone in the house?'

'No. My two children are asleep upstairs.' *God, I hope I didn't wake them when I screamed.*

'Someone will be with you in four minutes Madam. We have a patrol car in your location.'

I hang up and wait, frozen with fear. How the hell can anyone get in the house? *Of course, they can't.* Now he's seen me he'll be half a mile away. He'll know I'll call the police.

The front doorbell rings. What if it's him? Now I know why Americans have spy holes in their doors. I see a blue flashing light through the curtains, so it feels a safe bet that it's the police. I open the door with shaking hands.

'Mrs. Roseland?'

'Yes. Come in. Please.'

'You reported a prowler. Could you show us where you saw him?'

I take the two officers through the house and into the back garden.

'Here.' I wave in the general direction he came from. 'I saw him twice. Once he moved across the patio and then about three minutes later, I saw him move across the grass. He was crawling and wearing a mask.'

Both officers produce sturdy torches and flash their beams across my garden. I put the outside light on and remain in the kitchen, still in shock. *For heaven's sake. Get a grip.*

The young, fresh faced officer returns with something in his hand. A faint blush is rising on his cheeks. 'Is this yours Mrs Roseland? I found it on the lawn.'

He offers me a pair of my pink lace panties. I realise I'd forgotten to get the washing in earlier.

'Yes.'

The older officer returns to the kitchen. He looks like he's seen it all before. 'Would you be good enough to see if anything else is missing Mrs. Roseland? If you can remember what washing you put out.'

I follow him into the garden with a washing basket and gather the content of the line into it. It feels damp from the night air. I take a stealthy look around but there's no one to be seen. *What did you expect?* 'I'll be able to check better in the kitchen,' I tell him.

OMG, I put at least four pairs of panties and two bras on the line. There may even have been three.

The officers wait patiently while I sort the children's washing from my own. I'm not easily embarrassed but to sift my lingerie in front of two strangers feels weird. My hands are still shaking.

'I think there are two pairs of panties missing. Three with the one you brought in.'

'He dropped that one. Probably when he realised you'd spotted him.'

By now he could be doing unmentionable things to my underwear. Or maybe he's wearing it.

'Is there a friend you could ring Mrs Roseland? It might be good to have someone with you for an hour or two.'

I want to phone Jono but then reality kicks in and I remember it's over. I'd give anything for one of his cuddles right this minute. Married or not.

'Yes. I'll ring my friend Susie.'

'It might be good if she comes over. It'll settle you a bit, won't it? We'll stay until she arrives.'

I ring Susie but Greg answers the phone. I'm to the point. 'Knicker nicker in the garden. Any decent suggestions?'

'Kate. What the hell is happening?'

I give him chapter and verse and then put the kettle on again.

'I'll make you both a cup of tea, I tell the officers.' *Why do I feel like some sort of loony who needs a carer*? How can a prowler make me shake from head to toe? I find some digestive biscuits and throw them on a tea plate.

It's Greg who rings the doorbell six minutes later.

'Susie was ready for an early night. In her pyjamas.' He gives me a quick hug. 'What's going on officer?'

Why am I such a burden to my friends? And why the hell was some warped nutcase after my panties? He'd have got a shock if he'd been in Poppy's garden. I've seen her passion-killers and he sure as hell wouldn't want to wank over those.

At last, I'm in bed and it's over. Well, apart from the aftershock. Violated, that's how it feels. Yes, it feels like an earthquake has shaken my world. One minute I'm making a mug of tea, mulling over whether to murder a small smudge in my womb, and the next, my world tilts up-side-down and the police are on the doorstep.

Greg was a poppet, bless him. Susie rang and told me she'd come over if I needed her. 'Haven't I always told you your sexy underwear would get you into trouble? If you shopped at good old M&S no one would look twice at it.'

She has this way of bringing sense to any situation. The two police officers drank their tea and told me they'd keep an eye on the house overnight. That's a comforting thought. I might even catnap. The children, of course, have slept through the whole incident. As soon as they've gone, I convince Greg to go home. 'I'm fine. Really, I am.'

I read in bed for a while. I'm not sure how much of my book I'm absorbing but the pretence is comforting. Calm returns to the house and I can feel the contented breathing of the bricks. Silly, I know, but I often take comfort in the thought that this house watches over me and the kids.

The phone rings. I look at it and decide I'd better answer it. I put the receiver to my ear, and something breathes heavily; it just breathes into my ear. Man or beast, I couldn't tell.

'Hello. Who is this?' My heart rate rises again, and my mouth is dry. And still the breathing.

'Nice panties.' He sounds like he's talking through fabric. It's muffled and disguised. And then he sniffs. 'Umm...I could lick you all over. Bet you'd like that.'

I hang up. I'm going to be sick. I rush to the bathroom but take the phone off the hook as I pass.

This is the final straw. I switch the bathroom light on and reach into the bowl. As I'm mopping up, I think I hear a shower of gravel thrown at the window. Then another. The window is opaque glass so I can't see what's going on, but I make an informed guess. I listen. Maybe I'm mistaken. I turn off the light and stand in silence. I decide I've imagined it. I have a pee and return to the safety of my warm bed. I'm shaky and feel chilled. The heating is off, and I snuggle under the covers to get warm.

And then it starts again; this time it's on my bedroom window. It's gravel. It's unmistakably handfuls of gravel from the drive. But now I'm angry. Mostly with myself for feeling so scared but also with the bloody prowler who thinks he can scare me witless. I'm never one to play the victim for long. Anyway, what harm can a shower of gravel do? I'm locked inside and the police are keeping a watch on the house.

I march to the window and pull back the curtains and then I nearly faint. The black-clad, masked man is leaning on my garden wall with my lace panties held on one finger. He waves them at me like he is my best friend. I close my curtains and fall onto the bed as huge sobs start from somewhere very low. I tremble; my legs won't work. I crawl across the bed to the phone and dial 999 again. This time I'm hysterical and can hardly get out a coherent word.

'Madam. I need you to calm down so that I can help. I can't understand you.'

'Man with panties. Outside. Help.'

The response time was a credit to the Police Service. Almost before I find strength in my legs to stand, the doorbell rings and a police officer is calling through the letterbox.

'It's the police Mrs Roseland. Open the door please.'

I hear Hannah get out of bed. 'Mummy. What's that noise? What's happening?'

'Nothing Darling. Go back to bed before you get cold.'

'But I heard a noise. It's the police. And you screamed.'

'Hannah. Everything is under control and there's nothing for you to worry about. Honestly. I need to let the policemen in so please, pop back into bed.'

Is she likely to do as she's told? Of course not; she's her mother's daughter and she'll dig and delve until the truth comes out. She'll sit at the top of the stairs and listen.

I have a deja vu moment as I let the same two policemen back in my house. I flag up the fact that Hannah is awake and the need to speak with care. I whisper. I shake. I want to be sick again but hold on to my stomach. I can see my underwear flying like the Jolly Roger from some creep's fingers. There's nothing very jolly about how I feel now.

'Please go into the kitchen. I shan't be a moment.' The two officers do as I ask. 'Put the kettle on if you fancy another brew.' *That sounds a bit more like normality.*

I call Hannah's bluff and find her perched on the stairs, as expected. She's shivering and pale. 'Come on Humpy. It's back to bed for you.'

'What do those people want? Why did you let the police in?'

'They're just checking that everyone is tucked up in bed and you're not, are you? Come on sleepy head. Let's get you under the covers quickly. You're freezing. You shouldn't sit on the stairs Sweetie. Not in the middle of the night.' The scent of my daughter calms me. I can't be sure she'll stay in bed, but I've done my best. 'Try to get back to sleep.' I kiss her and return to the officers in my kitchen who have taken up my offer and the older one is already making tea.

'I should think this has shaken you up Mrs. Roseland. Can you think of anyone who might do this?'

'I try not to mix with perverts Officer. My address book is clean out of perverts.' I'm joking. I don't want to admit how shaken I am.

'We'll send for a female officer to spend the rest of the night with you. Would that make you feel safe Mrs. Roseland?'

'No thanks… although it's very kind of you to offer.' *I'm not a bloody wimp. I've dealt with worse. Steady. They're only trying to do their job.*

'If it's any consolation Mrs Roseland, these sorts of men rarely, if ever, harm people. They always run away after finding what they're looking for.'

'He certainly knows how to scare the shit out of me.'

'That's how they get their thrills. Scaring women'.

'He must be thrilled tonight.'

Hannah appears in her dressing gown with tussled hair and a face that says she isn't going to be fobbed off with fairy stories.

'A bit late for you to be up I'd have thought', said the fresh faced one.

'When you hear your mother scream in the night and police arrive it's hard to sleep,' she retorted. *Oh Lord. Is she like me or what?*

'I expect it is. But you know all sorts of things go bang in the night, and I expect it was a motorbike that backfired. Very noisy things, motorbikes.'

'But Mum doesn't usually scream at things like that.'

'Humpy... it's much too late for you to be up. Go back to bed. Please.'

'No. I'm sure your mother doesn't usually scream, but if you're deep in a lovely dream it can be very frightening. A motorbike backfiring or something like that. I think you'd be better off back in your warm bed, and we'll take care of Mum. I'm going to make her a nice cup of tea and then she's going back to bed too.'

Amazingly Hannah took his advice and after a quick hug with me she climbed the stairs. I eyed the mugs of tea and wondered if I broke open a bottle of red, they would judge me an alcoholic.

'We shall make reports about both incidents Mrs. Roseland and for the next week I shall add this address to the night patrol. Please call us if you have any more incidents but, in my experience, he's probably got designs on another washing line already. They're very hard to catch, these individuals, but when we do, they usually get a custodial sentence.'

'I can just about hack the washing line incident, but to throw gravel at my windows is really... spooky. He's taunting me. It feels personal.' *Is it something to do with that strange note?*

'I shouldn't think about it too much more tonight, Mrs. Roseland. We'll keep a close watch on the garden, so I suggest you try to get some sleep. I've asked for a patrol car to stay in the road for the next couple of hours. Not that I expect a return visit from him. They're all cowards. It's too risky to come back, you see.'

Great. I'm going to buy some big knickers in M&S tomorrow, that's for sure.

The next morning, I manage to make it to work. What kind of gook steals women's knickers? I had no idea why I was so scared but there had been a primeval fear that wasn't based on anything I understood. Man in the garden, doors locked, and police on their way. Was it so scary? But still it shook me to the core. I didn't think there would be any lasting damage with Hannah. The calm policeman was on the ball with his explanation, and she didn't even mention it this morning.

Chapter 16

Kate knew she'd been in foster care prior to her adoption by the woman she called Bitch-Mother, as she could remember the details of that traumatic time. She remembered her arrival at the new home and being told to call the strangers. Mummy and Daddy. But the dearth of information from her infant life, those years when she was too young to remember, had become her nemesis. She longed to find her birthmother to fill the chasm inside her. The not knowing where her family roots lay, had eaten away at her for as long as she could remember.

But Kate was a realist and had little expectation that she would one day fall into the arms of a loving birthmother. However, she was curious about the events that had taken her down such a perilous childhood path. She longed to know what genes had put her on this earth.

Kate knew that one day she'd take the plunge. When the time was right, she'd follow the clues and try to uncover her heritage. Searching out the foster mother could be key to her success.

During the years when she'd been happy and settled with Chris, and particularly when the children came along, everything about Kate's chaotic childhood had been put on hold. Chris and the children had quelled her needs and fed her soul in a way that allowed her to abandon her desire to start the search. But things were different now.

'If you leave this thing much longer Kate, your mother could be dead.' Susie was right. Susie was usually right. Even when they were at school it was always Susie who had top marks and won the prizes. 'You need a new stability. And you know

Greg and I will be there for you. Maybe knowing your background and finding the truth, could kill a few demons.'

Or land me with a few more. That's a risk I'm willing to make.

After losing Chris and living the nightmare of being a single parent, the old urge to find her roots had returned. It was like an itch that needed scratching, a toothache that nagged away until she could no longer ignore it. So, she decided, right or wrong she would start looking for her birthmother.

With encouragement from Susie, Kate made mental notes to aid her search, and on the chosen day she woke with a dry mouth and no appetite for breakfast. She'd eyed the children's cornflakes with disgust. A 'red letter day' Chris's Godmother would have called it. Kate could hear Juliet's dulcet tones in her head. *'Go on Kate. What are you waiting for? Go and find your mother.'*

But the chores of the morning diverted her musing.

'You're not having my Lego. It's mine.' Tom was puce and within an inch of shoving his sister into the fire hearth. 'Anyway, you can't build proper things. She can't, can she Mummy?'

'It never hurts to share Tom. I don't think you'd miss a few bits, do you?'

'See. I told you.' Hannah's eyes sparkled with triumph.

Tom passed some pieces of his precious Lego to his sister and promptly disappeared into the garden, probably to sulk for five minutes.

Single parenting gets no bloody easier.

Susie had offered to give the children their lunch so that Kate could have a clear afternoon for her maternal search. 'I'll take them to the cinema and then to a KFC for supper.'

'Yeah. We love Kentucky.' It was met with the children's approval.

That only left the morning to fill. Tom had been given a jigsaw for his birthday and Kate had promised to help him with it all week. Today was the day. Humpy wanted to play at a friend's house across the road, so it was the perfect opportunity for some time with her son.

As he'd unpacked the jigsaw with the enthusiasm of a Labrador puppy, Kate wondered what the consequences of her search might be. For her and for Tom and Hannah. Would it conjure up the Granny they'd never had? Or would she court yet another disaster that would have a negative impact on her family? Only time would tell.

And so, with over-arching concerns but a grim determination, that afternoon Kate drove to the village where her earliest memories began.

She'd known exactly how to find the cottage where she'd been fostered for eighteen months at the tender age of three. The village was one of the mellow-stoned, rural Cotswold communities much sought out by American tourists, and only six miles from her eventual home with Bitch Mother. Kate had often been back to the village, passing through it on her way to shop in Cirencester. But today it was different. Today she was there with intent. She'd spent years mulling it over and now was the moment.

The grey ribbon of rural road was dotted with Cotswold cottages, many with thatched roofs, pretty gardens and a proliferation of beech trees standing sentry over the ancient stones. The road led to a small square where the popular pub sat at the heart of the village. Here, she remembered, the local hunt had met during the winter months. She had a flash-back of dogs with long, wagging tails which were almost as tall as her. Scary.

She'd known there was a stone wall around the garden of the foster home, which sat on one side of the square. And it was that wall, despite the degree of difficulty for small hands, that she'd scaled like a mini mountaineer all those years ago. She'd plonked her backside on the flat stone at the top which was a perfect fit for a small bottom. And from there, she had watched the comings and goings of village life as her little legs hung aimlessly above the road. She had often scraped her knees on the rough stonework and used to spit on her hands to soothe them. Or she'd used dock leaves. Sometimes, she'd snagged her dress, but the rips never saw a needle and thread in a very over-crowded foster family.

Kate held fond memories of the foster-mother. Greying hair which she'd tucked in a scarf and knotted at the front, and a large, cream, wrinkled face on which she balanced dark-rimmed, National Health spectacles. Robust and ample bosomed, she'd filled the doorway of the cottage. Her cotton pinafore had concealed a bounteous stomach on which she'd rested her hands. Sometimes she'd sneak one of her better-half's fags and after puffing away only half of it she'd hide the butt in the geranium pots. She was so bad on her feet that she'd used a hazel stick, fashioned by her husband, to support her frame. But there was nothing frail else about her. Nothing had stopped her contribution to the ever-expanding family.

'Call me Gran,' she'd told the frightened little girl when she'd been dropped off. 'Everybody calls me Gran.' The man who brought her had taken leave with unseemly haste and Gran had proffered a sticky sweet which she'd dug from the depths of her apron pocket. 'If you're good, you can walk up to the garage with me tomorrow.' Kate had eyed her from behind the sofa. 'And we'll bring home Gramp's cigarettes,' she'd added. 'You can buy some sweets if you're good.'

There had been no specific bedroom offered to Kate. Just a vague explanation that, 'there's always room to sleep somewhere in this house, Ducky.' Before long, grown girls had returned home from work and school, bustling and arguing, crimping hair and fighting over makeup. They'd paid little attention to Kate.

'Another stray in the nest I see, Ma. Meat on Sunday then,' quipped Eddie, the only son in the brood. It was a family joke that foster-kids put food on the table. Oily overalls and smears of grease confirmed Eddie's apprenticeship to the local car mechanic. His grimed fingers never quite came clean, no matter how much carbolic soap was lavished on them. His sweaty armpits announced him long before his curly head appeared. He had eyed Kate's red hair, 'got a Ginger in the house then Ma?

'Get your filthy hands under that outside tap,' demanded Gran. 'And it's Friday. I want ten bob on the table, else there'll be no tea for you.' Gran ruled the house with an iron hand. 'And there'd better not be any more strays coming my way. I've told you enough times. Put a johnny on it if you can't keep it in yer trousers.'

Eddie had chuckled as he grabbed a towel and headed into the garden to wash. 'You won't have that kind of trouble from me Ma. Better tell the girls to keep their hand on their halfpenny though. That might help.' He went off, chuckling at his own joke.

'Go and watch him, little one.' Gran had coaxed Kate from behind the sofa again. 'The tap's a good place to play on hot days. Eddie will show you how to make the water spurt like a fountain.'

Most days it had been just Gran, Kate, and baby Lionel at home. Gran used to sweet-talk Kate down from her look-out on the wall with half-penny chews, and while they inevitably brought her from her perch, nothing stopped her re-scaling the wall within the hour. She stared up the road and into the distance. Hoping. Always wishing for something but not exactly sure what it was.

'Mind you don't scrape those sandals,' Gran had often called. 'And don't wake Lionel, I've only just got him to sleep.

Gran had a way of knowing all. She hadn't brought up eight children without learning a thing or two about what went on in kids' heads. 'Don't you be wasting any tears over what you can't change,' she'd told Kate. It had been good advice, as it turned out. 'Sooner you learn that the easier life will be.'

When bidden, Kate had climbed the cottage stairs and waited until someone pointed out her bed for the night. Later, a bevy of girls would arrive and fight over the available spaces. It was only years later that Kate realised the grown-up girls probably had boyfriends to stay, and so she was cast adrift to sleep elsewhere. She had never had a bed to herself. It was always shared with girls who had taken up all the space until she'd found herself hanging on the edge, petrified she'd fall. Or they'd shoved her in the middle where she'd nearly died of heat. They'd crept in late and smelt strange. And they'd smoked cigarettes. Those girls, who had frequently hung from the bedroom windows, shouted to boys and puffed clouds of smoke and hairspray into the air, were the bane of her little life.

But today was different. It would bear no resemblance to those fragile childhood days. When Kate arrived in the village, she was determined to make her quest successful. *Just a snippet of information would get me started.* She found a space in the pub carpark and pondered awhile, staring out of her windscreen. *And just what do you think you are going to say? 'Hello, I used to live here amongst the chaos known as the Oswald family.'* Maybe she'd pretend to sell something and engage the occupant in conversation. Or maybe she would go home. But she had never been a quitter.

Eventually she'd grabbed her courage in both hands and walked across the village square. Even the garden wall was still there, although now boasted a cascade of purple clematis which would have discouraged a small mountaineer. It crossed Kate's mind, as she'd tried to pluck up courage to knock on the cottage door, that it would have been a substantial fall if that little girl had missed her footing, all those years ago.

She'd eventually knocked and a woman in her forties answered with a smile.

'Can I help?'

'Eh...maybe.'

The woman waited.

'I'm looking for the family who lived here around thirty years ago,' she began. 'Oswald, I think they were called.'

'Ah, yes. I know who you mean but they've moved.'

Kate's heart plummeted into her rather smart designer shoes. All those years she'd thought about searching for her mother, and she'd waited too long. The foster family had gone, and with them the clues to her birth mother.

'Would you like to know where Mrs Oswald lives now?'

'She's still alive?' asked Kate.

'She's alive and kicking,' laughed the attractive lady. 'Annie is quite a leading light in the village community.'

'I'd love to have her address. Has she moved far?'

'All of two hundred yards. If you take the right hand fork out of the village, she's the first house on the left. Thyme Cottage. After the British Legion. You can't miss it.'

'Thank you so much. Sorry to bother you.'

This was better than Kate could have hoped for, but now, blind panic set in. What on earth was she going to say? Keep it simple, she'd told herself. Tell it like it is.

Thyme Cottage was a quintessential country cottage built of ubiquitous Cotswold stone. A metal gate led to an uneven stone pathway and the borders were a profusion of late summer flowers. The hum of bees filled the air. The green door of the house beckoned, and Kate rapped her knuckles on the shiny paint and waited. She hardly dared to breathe. Then she'd waited some more.

After a while a cheery voice was heard. 'Hello. Can I help you?' A lady appeared from behind the cottage.

'Oh. Hello. My name is Kate. Maybe I've got the wrong cottage,' she blurted. 'I'm looking for Mrs Oswald and I know she'll be... What I mean is...'

'She'll be a lot older than me?' The tall lady, who was fifty, or thereabouts, had snow-white hair scraped into a band.

Could be worse. She doesn't look like she'll bite.

'Well... yes. I suppose that's what I mean.' Kate gave a nervous laugh. 'Is Mrs Oswald in?'

A man joined them who'd clearly been busy in the garden. He rubbed soil from his hands onto his trousers. 'Hello. Don't think we've seen you before.'

'I'm looking for Mrs Oswald,' Kate repeated. 'I was fostered by her, years ago.'

'Were you now?' The tall lady stepped towards Kate and scrutinised her.

'You'd better come inside. I'm afraid I'm a bit grubby. Straight from the garden you see.' The man opened the cottage door and entered, scraping soil from his boots. Kate followed him and the lady inside. She had a dry mouth and an excited heartbeat drumming in her ears.

'What exactly,' asked the lady, 'do you think Mum can do for you?'

'I think she may hold the key to my roots.'

'I wouldn't be a bit surprised,' said the man who had a very kind face and a warm smile.

Kate

Chapter 17

The day I found my birthmother was not how I'd imagined it would be. For there she was before me. Tall, slim, and attractive and holding all the secrets of my past. There was no time to adjust. No time to prepare. She, the originator of my gene-pool was scrutinising me as if I was a bargain in a Christmas sale.

Clearly, she realised who I was at least a minute before the reality dawned on me. For her it was easy, but there were no tell-tale auburn curls, no clues for *me* to grasp. For I had come with low expectations, only to interrogate an elderly foster mother, and the reality was overwhelming. No wonder I was confused.

Was there an invisible thread that pulled me to the realisation that she was my mother? I have no idea, but it dawned like a meteor falling to earth. As I looked into the eyes of my long lost mother, I became that unwanted child again. The adult me was washed with emotions which seeped through my pores.

There was no doubt that she was shell shocked, too. And no wonder. While she had been tidying up her mother's garden, out of nowhere springs her abandoned daughter. Last seen twenty odd years before. I guess she had to assimilate the small child she'd put up for adoption with the adult before her. And there was no formulation for this meeting, and no rule book for either of us.

Would I have door knocked if I'd known my mother was going to greet me? Probably not. Umm...make that a yes. I probably would have.

'Mum and Dad are out at the moment,' she'd told me. George and I are trying to keep their garden up together.'

I look around but absorb nothing. My mind goes blank in the fear of the moment. 'Oh.' I swallow hard. I decide to make her say it. *Say, 'I'm your mother.' Go on. Let me hear you say it.*

I push a little, waiting for confirmation of my assumption. 'I know I was fostered in this village and... I want to find out where I came from. I must have arrived from somewhere. Surely it wasn't a gooseberry bush.

The woman smiles but her face is a mask. I have no idea where this is leading.

'We can certainly help you, Kate.' The kindly looking man spoke quietly.

My heartbeat races. Am I ready for this?

'Come in. Come inside,' the woman suggests.

I follow. Was I a lamb to slaughter? I'm led into a sitting room and offered a chair. After a pause I prompt her, 'you said you could help be trace my roots. I've waited a long time to hear someone say that.' I was hanging on tight to any tears.

'I can.' She'd hesitated nervously. I hope this is not too much of a shock but...I'm your birthmother. I'm Veronica and this is my husband, George. And you must be Kate.' She smiled as if it was a job interview. 'I know who you are because I've watched your childhood milestones with interest. I saw you catch the school bus and watched you push your doll's pram across the common. Yes, dear. You were mine, but for such a short time.'

I could not believe I was standing before my mother. I had prepared myself for various scenarios, but never this one. And her eyes were watery, filled with emotion. After my years of dreaming about her, here she was.

'But I'm not your father Kate. I think it best to clear that point.' It was an uncomfortable George trying to find a framework to move forward, and who could blame him for wanting to tidy away any misunderstanding. It was a little late for maintenance demands, but best got out of the way.

'Thanks for telling me.' *No genes pool there to juggle with then. Curiouser and curiouser, except I'm not bloody Alice.*

Veronica didn't meet my eyes but George was ready to grasp the situation and steer it into calm waters. 'Let's put that to one side then, shall we? Let's talk about you. Have you had a good life, Kate? I know Veronica has never stopped wondering how life treated you.'

Do we really want to open that can of worms, today? 'Can we leave my story for another day? I've waited a long time to know about my past; I've dreamed of finding you Veronica. I'm...sorry it turned out to be such a shock...for both of us. As you can guess, it's the last thing I expected.'

'I'm sure.' She smiled again but her eyes were distant.

'Perhaps you can fill in some of the gaps for me? Until my own children were born, I'd never known a blood relative. Kind of odd, don't you think?' *Don't embarrass her. Easy Kate. Take things easy.*

It was obvious that George adored Veronica. He struck me as the dependable sort; someone you could take your troubles to, and he'd halve them in a flash. *I had a man like that once.*

George looked at Veronica, encouraging her to grasp the reality of what was before her. He resembled a father spooning breakfast into a reticent child, as he gradually enticed her to engage. 'Off you go love. I'm here to help if you get stuck.'

Veronica imparted a disjointed account. It was a full on narrative with jumbled timelines. She appeared keen to tell me everything in one hit, hardly drawing breath once she was under way. It felt as though she believed that if she stopped, she'd never have the courage to finish the story.

I was only able to absorb a fraction of what I was told. I was dazed from the surprise of finding her and knew I'd struggle to unravel the information when I had time to reflect.

But it wasn't the string of details that mattered, I realised. *There would be another time to pick it all apart.* Today, it was about the massive tide of emotions floating in an ocean of sadness. It was a story of this woman when she was a young girl, making life-changing decisions. I dared to believe it was about love and separation, about hopes that were dashed and finding courage to do the right thing. I doubted Veronica had had an easy life, particularly when she was young.

From the many things she told me that day, I recognised her attraction to unsuitable men. *An unwanted gift she'd passed to me. At least I now have someone to blame.*

Veronica hadn't married until she was forty seven, having waited for George to get his divorce from a long-separated wife. I believe her late marriage was from choice, rather than lack of opportunity. There was a photo of her above the fireplace, taken when she must have been around twenty. *After she had me.* The photo showed a pretty, confident young lady ready to take life by the horns. I searched for any visible scars from giving me away but found none.

And how alike we are. I could now see where my red curls came from, and my mouth is an identical shape to hers. *She's got the same kick-ass spark in her eyes, too.* But Veronica told me her early life was clouded with bad-judgements and head-strong decisions. She sounded as if she'd been wilful as a teenager. She mentioned the Servicemen who were stationed close to her village with a twinkle in her eye.

And then she became impatient to finish her story.

'I tried to ignore the signs when I was carrying you. I was just eighteen and I was entangled with a married officer at the Army base where I was stationed.' *Bingo. A bloody married man was my father. Why are we both attracted to married men?*

'But you were soon hard to ignore.' She gave an uncomfortable laugh. 'Uniforms were unforgiving when it came to baby-bumps, and you were a big baby from about three months.' She gave a small smile before gazing out of the window. Had it been anyone else or any other conversation, I would have assumed she was a garden-lover. But this was a dark brown study taking her somewhere else and to a time long ago. I watched George for any sign of annoyance as the story unfolded, but there was none. He didn't appear the jealous type. He'd obviously heard it all before.

'I was dismissed from my post in the Women's Royal Airforce. When the bump appeared. There was no way to deny you were on the way, you see. And what a disgrace! Not you dear,' she added hastily. 'Me. Your father was rapidly posted abroad, and I never heard from him again. I arrived home to a mother who was livid. I was the bright one of the brood or so they told me, and I was in a mess of my own making.'

That rings a bell. I'm good at that, too.

I remember looking at her hands with their long, beautiful fingers and carefully polished nails. It was no wonder she wore gardening gloves. Lovely nails were something I hadn't inherited, having been a nail-biter for as long as I can remember. But for the first time in my life, I had a point of reference, some genetic similarity and I was looking at …yes, she was my mother. I could feel emotions bubbling up and it was only a matter of time before the enormity of what was unfolding spilt over into full blown tears. A whole lifetime was expanding like a concertina.

I liked her. Something about her called to my soul. There was a familiarity about her and yet she was a stranger. I had yet to touch her. I hadn't felt her skin or grasped the scent of her. Would I have infant memories of either?

George came up with an idea. 'What about a small sherry? I'm sure Mum wouldn't mind'.

Veronica's eyes lit up and she went to the sideboard to arrange her mother's glasses and decanter. 'We can call it a celebration, don't you think? How can I be so lucky that you've found me? It's much more than I deserve.'

'Nonsense. Don't ever say that.' George gave her a look which revealed a gentle possessiveness. 'I won't allow her to put herself down Kate,' he explained. 'She's a wonderful woman and I, for one, will cross anyone who says otherwise.'

I believed him and felt a small pang of envy at the closeness between them. *You only need to find the right man and you can have it too.*

If I'm honest, I'd been waiting for the answers surrounding my adoption. I wanted to hear how she gave me away and under what circumstances. How had she felt? Did she have maternal emotions or was I a parcel to dispose of as quickly as possible. Did she want to rid herself of me so that she could start her life where she'd left off. I was dreading the detail, yet desperate for the truth. I sipped sweet sherry with concealed disgust and embraced the essence of a happy reunion.

Eventually the revelation came.

'You obviously remember Mum...and living with the family.' Her eyes clouded. 'Or you wouldn't have found us. Silly me.' She looked to George for courage. 'I wanted to keep you Kate, but adoption was the only option back then for babies born out of wedlock. What a horrid phrase, isn't it? I've always hated it. It wasn't anything like it is today... no flat would have been allocated. No allowance provided by the government. No, my dear, you must believe me... it was tough to be a girl 'in trouble.''

Her eyes are not with us; they've gone to a dark place... 'I gave birth to you in a mother and baby home in Cheltenham. I was allowed to keep you for six weeks before your new adoptive parents came to take you away.' The dark brown study returned... 'Can you imagine feeding and caring for your baby for that long, and then having her snatched away by an authority who frowned on your 'bad ways'?'

I couldn't. I thought of having my first-born daughter snatched away from me, or darling Tom with Grandfer John's eyes and Chris's double crown. The idea was incomprehensible. But Veronica wasn't done yet.

'And then you came back to us, when you were three, all tussled curls and attitude. Your adoptive family had been through many problems, including the death of your adoptive mother. She had cancer. So, you found your way back to us and, if I'm honest, I believed you'd always be with me. I thought you'd grow up in the family.' More tears were forming, and I watched as they pooled and slid down her cheeks. 'I lost you twice, you see. I had to give you away again and it...it wasn't fair.'

I felt her pain and it was hard to bear. She'd loved me. I couldn't doubt that. George went to her and held her hand and she began again, with renewed strength.

'And one day, I knew you'd be old enough for me to tell you that I was your mother.' I noticed her blink in a vain attempt to stem her tears. 'I'm a silly thing. George, could you lend me your hankie?'

George had mopped her eyes with a snowy, cotton handkerchief. 'Come on my love. The time for tears is over. Your daughter has come back to you.'

'I had no option but to give you up Kate.' Her large brown eyes held a lifetime of tears and they continued to slide, unchecked, as she dabbed them with George's hanky.

'Tell her what you told me. Tell her about Fred.'

Veronica took a deep breath and two sips of sherry.

'Your first adoption was with Fred and his wife Sally who already had a daughter of their own. They couldn't have a longed for second child. It was to them I gave you when you were six weeks old. They adored you. They brought a wicker basket lined with sprigs of summer flowers and a blanket that Sally had crocheted while waiting for you to be born.' Veronica's tears continued to run unchecked down her pretty face. 'They took you away in it and I watched, helpless and desolate. But I justified it by telling myself you would have a better life with them. And you would, if not for her untimely death. She was only thirty eight when she died.'

Shit. I had a sister I don't remember. Where can she be now?

'How old was she? My sister. Do you know what happened to her?'

'I don't Kate. She was called Louise. I'm so sorry.' Veronica was calmer and the tears were slowing. 'When Sally died, you were only just three and Fred contacted me and asked if I could take care of you while he sorted his life out. Mum agreed to do the fostering while I continued to work and so, that was how you came back into the family.

'Let me top up your sherry dear.'

And there was more. 'Then, when you were five, completely out of the blue, Fred asked us to take you back to him. He said he'd arranged for a second, private adoption, and I was devastated. I don't think private adoptions exist today, but they were quite common in the sixties.' She looked at George as if for a battery recharge and yet more inspiration.

George used his hankie to blow his nose and I realised he was affected by the sadness and unfairness of the details, too.

Veronica was ready to continue. 'The request came in a letter to Mum. Fred told her he'd decided to have you adopted by wonderful people. He said he'd found the perfect family for you. And we were to take you back to him so that you could be passed to your new parents.'

Now I was the one getting tearful. Memories came flooding back. Fred. Yes, Daddy Fred. 'He promised he'd come and take me home... I remembered him, he'd promised to come and fetch me. I could smell the cigarettes he smoked. 'And he said he'd bring me a doll in a pink dress in a box. So, I sat on the wall, and I waited. For so many weeks I waited.' I grabbed some tissues from my bag.

Poor George, surrounded by two weeping women when all he wanted to do was sort out the in-law's garden.

 'Oh Kate.' Veronica was visibly shaken.

My head was a jumble. There was so much to absorb. I was wondering why I didn't remember Veronica. I could only visualise Gran and the noisy big girls and baby Lionel, and then it dawned on me, she was one of those girls who smoked cigarettes and called to boys through the bedroom windows.

George went into the kitchen and returned with two bowls of crisps. 'We don't want the sherry going to our heads, do we?'

No, we don't. I've got to drive home.

I began to wonder how much further this would take us. I noticed Veronica had stopped crying when she gave me a plaintive look.

'I tried to stop it you know. Your second adoption. I went to the court in Gloucester to oppose it, but I was told I had given up all rights to you when you were six weeks old. Can you imagine? I was distraught. It would be different these days, of course.'

I thought she might start crying again at the mere reminder of the pain. But for me there was a kind of redemption, a realisation that someone wanted me and was prepared to fight, even though she lost me.

'I never knew,' I tell her. *Stupid. Of course, you never knew. How could you?*

'Do you remember when we met you in Stratford Park? It was about a year after you left us. Your new adoptive mother was watching you go up and down on the slide when you suddenly spotted us sitting under a tree having a picnic. You ran to us and sat down on the grass. What happened next scarred me for life. I watched your new mother march across the grass, grab you by the arm and pull you away. Then she slapped your legs and you burst into tears. Obviously, you had no idea what you had done wrong.

I didn't remember but could visualise it. Tears spilled again for that little girl with all the curls and the attitude.

'What about a stroll around the garden Kate? Mum's proud of her lilies, isn't she dear? Not that she can do much in the borders these days. She suffers with bad arthritis.'

Veronica looked relieved. 'What a good idea. We seem to spend most of the summer doing this garden. It's much too big for Mum and Dad but they won't hear of moving to somewhere smaller.'

George gathered up the sherry glasses and took them to the kitchen.

We wandered the crooked stone pathways and oohed and aahed at the flowers. My head was racing, and I tried to remember if I had anything else I needed to ask. Suddenly, out of the blue, Veronica said, 'Maybe we could meet up again next week and... perhaps meet your children? What do you think? We only live a mile away from here, Kate.

'I think we should ask Kate if she sees us as fit people to be introduced to her children. How do you feel about that Kate? Is it all moving a bit fast?'

Yes, it is. I've had no time to think. What the hell will Susie make of it? I gulp. I try to get my head around it. *What will I tell my children? What would they call them -Granny and Grandpa?*

I made a snap decision. I'd waited longer than anyone I knew to have a proper family, and I wasn't going to hesitate now. 'That would be great. I could try to get a couple of days off work, and we could do some real catching up.'

'That would be perfect. Maybe we should leave the children for a week or two,' Veronica mused. And then she touched me. My mother touched me, and her hand shot sparks through my entire body. I turned to look at her and she enveloped me in her arms.

'You have no idea how I've dreamed of this day Kate. Did I tell you I called you Susan? Susan Joy, to give you your full name.'

We all laughed. 'I've answered to many names before, but never Susan!'

We said goodbye, but this time there was no heartbreak. We exchanged phone numbers and addresses and agreed to meet soon.

Chapter 18

Kate

I had more to process than any brain should be deluged with. A birth mother who wanted to have a relationship, a baby growing inside me who was due to be obliterated and a stalker/gook who liked scaring the shit out of me. Then there was Jono. Oh, and I still had to be a good mum and hold down my job.

I didn't want Veronica and George to be privy to my problems. I wanted them to know the best me. I suppose we all want that when we meet new people. And this was my newly found mother, so it was extra important. I certainly didn't want to give them even a glimpse of the dirty secrets of Jono Symonds, or stalkers.

I had somehow recovered from the night-time antics of a gook in my garden. Luckily, daylight had brought a dose of reality and the fear dissipated like water down a plughole. How scary could it be?

However, the issue of my baby was not resolved.

'You can't let the actions of a narcissistic idiot impact your decision to terminate this baby, Kate. Please don't do that.' It was Susie at her most vociferous.

'If anything, Jono's behaviour has made me more determined. I've changed the clinic time, so we won't have to cope with him tugging me into his car to prevent me having the op?'

'It could well have happened. Or worse.'

'Can you still come with me at 9.30?'

'Of course. I've set the whole day aside to make sure you're OK.

I had to admit to a growing desire to share my baby problem with Veronica, despite my good intentions. Maybe another perspective from a woman who knew all about unwanted pregnancy could have helped. But pride prevented me telling them. I wanted them to see a widow who had survived a traumatic couple of years, but who was now on the road to recovery. Nowhere in the blossoming relationship with my mother was there a space for the farce that was Jono Symonds. And so, Susie and I ploughed on together to sort the fragile issue I'd landed myself with.

On the appointment day we'd taken the children to school and went in Susie's car to the clinic. Then, it was me alone who had to deal with the gruesome event. And I never want anyone I know to have to go through it. It was a chilling, humiliating experience, despite lovely staff who'd done their best to put me at ease.

I had the necessary interview with a medic, of course, and signed the paperwork. It was at that point I realised there was no going back. As I lay with my legs in stirrups and my head all over the place, I was given a light anaesthetic which sent me to a soft, cloudy place while the little blob was dealt with. I was ashamed of what I'd done. I would never forgive myself. But it was over.

Susie insisted I went to her house for the day. We were both afraid Jono would harass me if I went home. He'd want to ensure I hadn't kept the original appointment which had been for 1.30pm.

So, in was in Susie's spare room that I'd fallen into a deep sleep. It was surprisingly dreamless and conscience free. There would be plenty of time for guilt and regret.

A few days later, after meeting Veronica for coffee and still feeling sad about the baby, I'd decided to decorate the kitchen to take my mind of things. I hadn't touched a paint brush since Chris had died and it felt like a step in the right direction. Jono's phone calls and violence had taken their toll on me, but I'd convinced myself he'd get sick of it eventually.

I had a few days off work to recover from the termination. The day before I was due back, I had done some chores around the house and picked up endless toys and detritus which were scattered around. I had a couple of bills to pay before I went to buy the paint for the kitchen and decided to make a cup of tea before my trip to town. Just as the kettle boiled, the doorbell rang, and I was blindsided to find Jono on my doorstep. He didn't speak; he walked right past me and into the kitchen.

'Come in why don't you?'

'Are you trying to wipe me from your life?'

'Bloody right I am,' I shot back at him.

'But Kate, if we are going to be together then you need to be patient. Give me a little time. Until I sort my marriage out.'

'How many times do I have to tell you? You won't leave your wife.'

He started to pace the kitchen floor and my eyes followed his strutting. He gave me a slightly uneasy feeling. 'What the hell is the matter with you? How did you know I'm at home today?'

'Kate...Katie...I know your every move, my darling. How can I not watch over the woman I love? And we will be together.' He leaned on the kitchen surface.

'You've not done it Katie. Tell me you haven't binned our baby.'

'Jono this isn't an easy decision...'

'Tell me you haven't.' He continued to pace; his face hardened and he was getting closer to me with each step. He grabbed my arm.

'Get off me. No, I'm still trying to decide...' I lie.

'At least *you* have a choice. But me, I wasn't worthy enough to even be told about it. Or so it seems.'

'But our relationship was over when I found out. I'm the only one who can make the decision. You must see that.'

'What I see is a scheming little bitch who wants to murder my child. In cold blood.'

'Please Jono. Don't make this more difficult than it already is. I'm in bits. The other night I had the most awful shock. The police were here and...'

'Poor little you. Had a fright, did you? Lost a few pairs of knickers? You love me so much, yet you can't even recognise me in the dark? Dear oh dear. Poor little Katie.'

Now I'm in full blown shock and sit on the bar stool before my legs give way. I can't even form words to express my disgust. It was him? *He scared me half to death as payback. OMG. What can I expect when he finds I've aborted the baby?*

'Get out. Get Out. And never come back.'

Chapter 19

Kate 10 months later

He's in there. He lurks behind that door, an impediment to my sanity. His pheromones are seeping through varnished wood and claiming the air I breathe. I'll see him soon enough. There he'll be - Adonis in the dock. And there I'll be, on oath and a shadow of my former self.

They tell me he's dangerous but what if I still want him? What if his sensual smile melts me to a puddle? What if? What if? Hey, stop this right now. I must be sick in the head. After all he's done to my family, what the hell is wrong with me? I won't look at his hands; their fine-fingered softness, pristine cuticles, and faultless nails that once stroked firecrackers across my body, could undo me. Remember, those hands also lit the match. Think how he watched from his delectable eyes while flames blistered my life.

I tap a slow digital beat on the wooden bench, counting the minutes before I face my demons. I'm probably annoying the hell out of my solicitor. Foolishly, I want to carve my name in the succulent wood panelling that adorns the walls of this ancient building. I want to mutilate its perfection and intercept its heady fragrance of polish that some poor cow has rubbed into it since she can't remember when. *Kate Roseland was here.* How good would that look?

I flex with dog-like pleasure, chafing against the wood, scratching like a terrier to de-stress my shoulders blades. I notice the looseness of my rings. I have pianist's fingers at last. I always wanted pianist's fingers. Although I wish my backside was still the 'luscious orbs' he couldn't keep his hands off.

Now I'm a 'bony prominence', according to Susie. And there was me thinking I was Liz Hurley.

He never stopped harassing me. How wrong I was to think he'd get sick of tormenting me. He still phones, usually in the middle of the night. He door knocks but I never let him in. I still miss him. My solicitor has sent warning letters telling him to stay away from me, but he doesn't.

I haven't dressed to impress him today. He loved me in purple. He said it turns my muddy-red curls to burnished gold. That's a load of bollocks, but he loved to talk like that. He loved to sweet-talk me and boost my confidence. Sadly, it's addictive. Danger, danger, defence mechanism needed.

Susie chose my outfit for today. I'm slightly uncomfortable if I'm honest, navy blue has never been my colour, and I never wear a matching skirt and top. I'm a mix and match kind of girl. But Susie insisted on the white blouse, too. 'You need to look prim. You know, the sort of woman a man wouldn't cross the road to get a better look at.'

Susie's already given evidence. She'll have been magnificent. Calm, organised Susie will have told the

court what a monster he is. I don't think I'll ever shed the guilt of my life choices, as long as I live. My children and I nearly died, and it was all because of my poor judgement. I keep making the same mistakes.

It's hot as hell in here; why doesn't someone open a window? No wonder I can't think straight. I uncross my legs and stretch my skirt over my knees. I check my watch for the umpteenth time and notice the usher who lurks within eye contact. Why doesn't she get some air in here? Do your job. And don't look at me like I'm a dropped stitch in a charity-jumper. Snooty cow. You have no idea what I've been through, so don't judge me. Actually, if she reads the local paper she'll probably know everything about my lousy life.

I won't look at him. Yes, that'll piss him off. I've changed over the months and God knows I needed to, but what if I still want him? What if the chemistry zings around the court like a tennis ball? Fifteen love. Thirty love. After all, it wasn't long ago my knees zeroed to jelly under his touch. But now I know him for what he is, has he lost his magnetism? I doubt it. 'Their eyes met across the crowded court.' Classic Mills and Boon. Shit! This isn't the way to go. This is real. Nail him. Get him put down for life.

I slide a tissue from the three packets I've brought in case I cry. I hear my name and stand like a robot. Now I'm walking behind the woman; she's tall and official-looking, silent, and sombre. Bet she doesn't have someone gagging for her at home. She leads me through the varnished door and into.... God knows what. Something has deprived my lungs of sustenance. The air is taut with expectation, for it's in here peoples' lives unravel like a ball of string. In here, reputations are shredded like butcher's mince, and it's me in the shredder today.

I'm not looking for him, but I can sense the stare. I scan the public gallery. Susie's there, wearing her crimson velvet hat with the floppy brim. She said it would cheer me up. I'm under instruction to think of it as a ray of hope in a sea of despair. She's imaginative, my friend Susie. And she'll be watching me for the smallest sign of weakness. Just before we left for court, she had some advice.

'The bastard nearly killed you and the kids. He's a phyco. Katie, Katie, please see him for what he is. You've had your clitoris in your headspace for too long'.

Harsh, I know, but everyone needs a Susie.

I trip on a step and then I read from a laminated card. Truth? Oh yes, I'll be truthful. The prosecuting QC stands and looks at me.

'Ms Roseland.'

I eye a glass of water with enthusiasm usually reserved for red wine.

'Could you confirm that the prisoner in the dock is known to you as Jonothan Symonds?'

This is it. I lift my head to the court and follow the line of minions until I see him. My heart catches in my throat, despite resolutions made. He's in a navy suit and tie. It's only his work-look for non-biking days, but the pearly-whiteness of the shirt does it for me. Virginal? Hardly. My knees scream for support and my hands start an annoying shake. I grab the glass of water to my left and the content hardly touches the sides of my rasping throat.

'He is.' *Should that have been 'he is your honour?' No, I think that's only for the Judge.'*

'Thank you. Could you confirm that you had a sexual relationship with Mr Symonds between March and November 1991?'

I gulp. *Is that what it was? A sexual relationship? And I thought he was the love of my life.*

'Yes.' It's a pathetic squeak but the best I can offer. *I don't think I'm doing very well at this.* I glance at the usher and proffer the empty water glass. *I feel hot. Maybe I've caught chickenpox from Susie's youngest.* I've missed something the QC said.

'I'm sorry. Could you repeat that?' I ask.

'Ms Roseland. I know this has been a traumatic time, but I need you to take your mind back to the fire. The fire that destroyed your home on November 19th last year. Do you have clear recollections of the event?'

'I do.....Yes....Yes I do. I do.' *Hell. I'm marrying the bloke now.*

'Then could you tell the court about the events leading up to the fire.'

Here we go. I've told the story a million times; I've told police and fire officers, solicitors, and insurance bods. Now I've got to do it all over again while those eyes in the dock question my every word. Remember, he tried to kill the children. That should sort me. To say nothing of what he put me through. And then there was the rape. But was it rape? If I'm honest he could have taken my soul without asking. For God's sake concentrate.

I look at him - in that silk shirt that needs ripping from his perfect, muscle-laden chest. *Did he hurt me? Maybe. Take me to shuddering orgasm. Yes. Stroke me until I could hardly speak for pleasure. That as well. But hurt me? He did scare me half to death though...and we could all have died.*

Damn. I've missed something else. I look at the QC and try to imagine him with no clothes on. Isn't that what they tell you to do if you're scared? It doesn't help. He's old, grey, wrinkled and...

'Ms Roseland?'

I need to focus. Water arrives and I gulp with the grace of a camel.

'We're waiting Ms Roseland. Tell us in your own words.'

OK. I can do this. I glance at Susie who smiles encouragement. The brim of her hat jiggles as she nods. She's like a lone poppy swaying in a breeze.

'It was a Wednesday. Just an ordinary day, really. The children went to school, and I was at work when my neighbour called to say a man was in my garden. "Prowling around," was how she put it.' *I knew. Even before I got home, I knew it was Jono.* I glance at the court. 'Of course, I went home to see what was going on....' my handshaking is getting worse. *Clasp them together, quickly. Come on, spit it out. They need to hear it. And whatever you do, don't look at him....* 'I found Jono Symonds sitting in the lavender border, smoking a cigarette. *He looked like a nineteen fifties bad boy. Moody, mean and totally fuckable.* 'I was surprised because I'd never seen him smoke before.' *Or sit in a lavender bed.*

'And had you ended your relationship with Mr Symonds at this point?'

'It was about six weeks after I'd told him our affair was over. I didn't know he was married you see. He lied about so many things.

'Did you have any other contact with Mr. Symonds during those six weeks? Before you found him in your flower bed?'

'Yes. He rang me at all times of the day and night. One day when I took the children to school, he was standing by the school crossing. He had a Mickey Mouse mask on and was holding a placard.

'What sort of placard?'

'It said, 'I love you Kate.''

'Anything else you'd like to tell the court Ms Roseland?'

'He started befriending my children.'

'How did he befriend your children?'

He was a sneaky little shit, that's how. 'I'd been very careful that my children didn't know about the relationship.' *But not careful enough, as it turned out.* 'They were still coming to terms with the death of their father.' *Don't dwell on Chris. What would he make of all this? He would have expected me to care for his children and I've turned out an unfit mother.* I reach for the empty water glass. 'Could I have more water please?' A jug arrives with a fresh glass that's been taken from the judge's desk.

'I wanted to be sure where our relationship was going before I allowed them to be aware of it. But they did bump into him on the odd occasion.'

'And when was that?'

'Sometimes he called in for coffee in the school holidays. He impressed my small son with a huge motorbike he owns.

Hannah was more cautious around him, but then he enrolled his own daughter into her Brownie pack. Hannah immediately wanted to accept an invitation from his daughter to go to his house for tea. That really freaked me.'

'I see. And did you allow this contact?'

'No. Not at first. I told Hannah we were going somewhere on that day. Next there was a written invitation sent to the house. I think it was the following week.'

How low is that? Using children to get what you want.

'And then, what happened?'

'Eventually....' I gulp some more water and look towards Susie. She nods the poppy in my direction which lightens the mood. 'After a phone call from his wife, I let Hannah go to tea at Jono's. Peer group pressure can be very strong you know.' *Don't justify yourself. He's the one in the dock, not you.*

'And did any harm come to your daughter?'

'No. She had a great time and wanted a reciprocal arrangement the following week, which I agreed to.'

'Did you see Mr Symonds on either of these occasions.'

Oh yes. I saw him everywhere. A flash of grey suit entering the dry cleaners; a man hurrying for a bus with a briefcase; and every bloody leather-clad biker this side of Tokyo, looked like Jono.

'Yes. He brought my daughter home and collected his own child from my house the following week.'

'Did he threaten you in any way?'

'Depends on the definition of threaten. I told him to stop pestering me. To stop using Hannah. I told him I'd go to the police if he didn't. He laughed at me and said I'd never be free of him. He said if you really love someone, you'll go to any length to have them.'

'Did you take that to be a threat?

'Not at that time. I was struggling with my own emotions. The shock that he had a family. All the lies...' . *My legs are giving way. I think I'm going to faint.* 'Please could I sit? I'm very hot and...

'Usher. Attend to Ms Roseland please.'

The usher hovers. He hands me a tissue and indicates a chair. I test my legs and then sit. I try to rise. *Wait. Not yet. I'm sure my legs aren't working. Give them another minute or two.* I sit and scrutinise the jury. *Don't look at Susie. Disappointment from Susie would be one step too far.*

'Are you able to continue Ms Roseland?'

Yes. Let's get this over and done with. I stand and sip from the glass of water. *If I drink much more water, I'll need a pee.*

'Ms Roseland?'

'Yes. I feel better. Sorry.'

'You said your neighbour called you and you found Mr Symonds "sitting in the lavender border, smoking." Did he give any explanation for his strange behaviour?

'Not really. He kept saying how sorry he was and that he'd leave his wife. I didn't believe him. To be honest, I didn't want him to leave his family. I told him he had responsibilities.'

'And what happened next?'

'I invited him in.' *Because I'm a prat.* 'I thought a cup of tea might calm him down. I still wanted to trust him you see.'

'And did it? Did tea calm him down?'

'No. He kept trying to touch me. He wanted me to change my mind. To take him back. When I said I doubted I could trust him again he said, 'I could make you trust me. I could make you do anything.' That was scary. I'd mostly seen the kind, loving Jono. Never like this.'

'Did he harm you in any way?'

'He left bruises on both my arms. I think by mistake. He grabbed me a couple of times to make me listen. He seemed agitated. Not himself.'

'And did he leave the house without further incident?'

'No...he tried to drag me to the sofa...he wanted to take my clothes off. He wanted...sex.' *I can't look at the jury. I feel a slut. A woman who's had a passionate affair with another woman's husband.*

'And did he succeed?'

'Yes.' *I fancied the hell out of him. I was an easy touch.*

'I see. And would you describe what happened as consensual sex?'

'Yes... It was consensual.' *Does all this go in the newspapers?*

'Was this the same day as the fire?'

'Yes.'

'Could you give more details Ms Roseland?'

I've started to nibble my nails. Susie warned me not to do it. She said I look like a lost kid when I bite my nails. Here goes. I look at the judge. 'There's something I need to tell you Your Honour.'

The Judge removes his glasses and looks at me.

'I'm not Ms Roseland. I'm *Mrs* Roseland, widow of Chris Roseland and proud to carry his name.'

'I apologise Mrs Roseland. Could the court record be amended appropriately?'

Something about speaking Chris's name calms me. It's been bugging the hell out of me. 'Ms' conjures up hippie types who don't know which way out to wear their clothes; saddos who haven't been married or jolly lesbian types. Well, it does to me. And I'm certainly none of those. I spot Susie in the second row of the gallery. Unfortunately, I also spot a gaggle of reporters, presumably already twisting my words for effect.

'Mrs Roseland?

'Sorry. Could you repeat that?' *I've done it again.*

'Would you tell the jury about the fire, later that day, Mrs Roseland.'

That's done it. I've looked at Jono and the bastard winked. His signature wink. I can't believe the cheek of him. Can a body melt into a puddle like ice-cream? No. Pull yourself together Kate. You've faced worse than this in your life. Pretend Bitch-Mother's in the dock. You'd be strong then, wouldn't you?

I look at the jury for the first time. And I tell them. 'He called that night when the children were in bed. It was after nine o'clock. He phoned me first and said if I didn't let him in, he'd wake the children and smash a window to get inside. He also said if I rang the police, he'd be waiting somewhere else. Another time. He said he only wanted to talk.' I gulp the water but don't take my eyes off the jury. There's a studious young man in the second row with glasses. He looks intense, as if he's listening to my every word. There's also the token black face in the front row. She looks sweet. The homely-mama type. She'll be on my side.

'And did you let him in?'

'Yes.' I clear my throat. 'Yes. I let him in. I didn't want my children woken. I tried to ring my friend Susie, but she didn't pick up and then he was...well, he was in my kitchen. I made him a cup of coffee and said something like, "why don't you leave me alone?" He laughed. He told me he would never leave me alone. When I reminded him about his wife and family...*OMG, she's probably in the public gallery. How can I repeat what he said about her?*

'Yes Mrs Roseland?'

'He said that they were not important to him. That he'd "get rid of them".

'What did you take that to mean?'

'I wasn't sure.'

'What happened then?'

'He asked me if I was still carrying his baby. Apparently, he'd called at my house on the day I went to the clinic for a termination and found I was out. It made him suspicious and very angry.'

'And were you still carrying his baby?'

'No. But I lied. I'd already had a termination.

'And then?'

'He looked at me and knew I was lying. I'm not a convincing liar and he just knew. I was frightened of what he might do.

'What did he do next Mrs. Roseland? You say you were frightened. Did you ring the police?'

'No. I told him I needed to check the children.'

'So, you left him in your kitchen while you went upstairs to check that your children were sleeping? Is that correct?'

'Yes. And they were. I went to the bathroom and tried to think of a way to get him out of my house. The problem was…I didn't want anyone knowing what a prat I'd been. You know…for letting him in in the first place.'

'How long were you upstairs?'

'More than five minutes. I was scared to go back down but knew if I didn't, he'd come up to see what I was doing.

'And when you went downstairs, what happened then?'

'He showed me a knife from his pocket. It was only small, it folded like a penknife. I asked him why he had it and he said, 'in case you're silly.'

'What did you take that to mean Mrs Roseland?'

'I...I guessed he was going to rape me while my children were asleep. I was still bleeding from the termination.'

'And did he?'

Don't look in the dock. He might wink again. Don't you dare!
'Yes. Yes, he did.'

'You let him into your house, and he raped you. Is that correct?'

'Yes.' It's a squeak again. I cough to regain my voice. I look at the jury. 'He raped me. Then he left.'

'And could you tell the court what happened next?

'I...I cleared up the kitchen and took a hot shower. I checked my children hadn't been disturbed by the shouting and I had a glass of wine. I was pretty shaken up.'

'You didn't ring anyone? A friend, a family member perhaps?'

'Yes. I rang Susie. My friend Susie. I told her what he'd done.'
I can't believe all this is being aired like bad rubbish. I'm a dustbin and they are emptying me, piece by piece. She told me to go to casualty, but I refused.'

'I see.'

'She wanted to ring the police for me, but I talked her out of that, too.'

'And why didn't you wish to report this crime?'

This is dangerous territory for me. Hang onto the waterworks for God's sake. 'I.... I felt dirty and ashamed. Ashamed that I'd been such a fool and let him into my house.'

'Mrs Roseland. Later that evening your house was set on fire. Is that correct?'

'Yes.'

'How did you first realise that the house was on fire?'

'I noticed the smell of smoke. It was coming from the garage end of the house, and I thought someone must have lit a bonfire, even though it was dark.'

'And what happened then?'

'I looked through the conservatory window and saw it. The garage was alight and there was a strong smell of petrol. Flames were licking up the walls and I realised the children were in danger. Hannah's bedroom is above the garage.

'What happened then Mrs. Roseland?'

'I rang 999 and then Susie and Greg. I rushed to get the children. *I'm not feeling great.* I gathered them in their duvets and brought them downstairs, one at a time. By then the smell of smoke was strong inside the house and we tried to leave...' *this is where I'm going to cry. Don't let him see you cry.*

'And what happened next?'

'Um…as we attempted to leave through the front door, I realised it was locked. I searched for keys. I was sure I'd left them in the door. By this time, I was beyond frantic.' *I notice a member of the jury has their eyes shut. Wake up! Hear me! I try to refocus.* 'I headed through the dining room, pulling the children with me…and found the conservatory door was locked too, and that key was also missing. By now the children were crying, hysterical with fear, and I was on autopilot. *I try another gulp of water and seek out the poppy. It is still waving.* I realised that the back door was our only option, but there was no key in that lock, either. The enormity of being locked in a burning house was crippling my thought process.

'What happened next?'

'Susie and Greg arrived in their car. They could see the fire and saw through the window that I was panicking. They tried the doors from the outside and said I should open the window and they would help us out. *This is the toughest bit. I can see it all as if it was yesterday. Blind fear, that's what it was.*'

'So, all three door keys were mysteriously missing, and the doors were locked?'

'Correct.' I'm nail-biting and looking at my shoes.

'Then what did you do?'

'I tried the windows. They are all triple glazed, plastic windows and I always keep them locked. But the keys were not where I keep them in the corner of the windowsill. They had been removed, too.' *I have that shaky knee feeling again.* By now I'm in blind panic,' I tell the jury. 'I'm on the phone to 999 again and they say the fire-engine is two minutes away. *I gulp some water to ease my dry mouth. How many more times must I relive this nightmare?* I straighten my back and look directly at the Judge. I want him to feel my panic and understand the enormity of believing your children will burn to death.

The QC continues. 'Could you tell us what happened when the Fire Service arrived?'

'They got to us just in time,' I continue with renewed strength. 'The fire had burnt through the kitchen wall and smoke was beginning to choke us. My children were hysterical.'

'How did the Fire Service rescue you?

'They smashed through the French doors in the conservatory.'

'And what was the condition of you and your children?'

'We'd all suffered from smoke inhalation. My children were kept in hospital overnight, but I was discharged. I went home with my friend Susie as my house was unsafe.'

'So let me get this straight. You and your two sleeping children were locked in a burning house with no means of escape?'

'That's right.' *I can the smell smoke. I can see the flames and* … large teardrops have formed and plopped onto my hand. I dab them with tissues, but it doesn't stem the flow.

'And do you have any idea Mrs Roseland, who may have started the fire?'

'Jono Symonds was watching it burn from the garden. He was leaning against the shed.

'You saw Mr Symonds in your garden?'

'Yes. As the fireman released us from the burning house, he was watching. I asked the fire service to call the police. He needed punishment you see. For what he'd done to my family.'

'And what made you think Mr Symonds started the fire? Did you see him do it. Did he tell you so?'

'No. He said nothing. He just watched. And...'

'Please carry on Mrs Roseland.'

'He dangled my house-keys on his finger. They have a distinctive star attached to them. I knew they were mine. He wanted me to see them.'

'Did Mr Symonds make any attempt to flee the scene?'

'No'

'How do you think Mr Symonds acquired your keys?

'I think he took all the door keys, and probably the window keys from downstairs, while he was in my house earlier that night. When I went upstairs to check on the children, he was alone in my kitchen.' *I wonder if I sound truthful.* He must have locked the front door from the outside when he left. I didn't notice. I was mad with rage after he'd raped me.'

'Could you tell the jury what happened when the police arrived?'

'Yes. They had a conversation with one of the firemen and then they arrested Jono. I believe they took my keys as evidence.'

'No further questions m'Lord.'

There's a woman in the public gallery who looks like Bitch-Mother. God help me, there surely can't be two of her. Why does Bitch-Mother always come to mind when I'm stressed? Why do I remember every detail of my years under her cruel regime when life hits rock bottom?

I drift into memory mode and its bedtime with Bitch-Mother. First a bath, where I was scrubbed with Dettol, followed by bed amidst warnings "don't wet the sheets unless you want dealing with in the morning". I've always known her physical and psychological cruelty has taken its toll, for how many ten year olds try to take their life with a gun?

'Mrs Roseland?' *How long since I answered a question?*

'Er... yes?'

'Would you like a five minute break?'

'Thank you.'

I'm escorted to the lavatory like a criminal. No speaking to anyone and no time to contemplate how I was doing. *Did the jury believe me? Did I come across as credible? Time would tell.*

I continued to ponder Bitch Mother as I sat on the loo. How she'd made my nose bleed when she threw me against the cupboard door. The fateful day the gun lay on the floor, witness to the sorry tale. I sit longer than necessary on the lavatory. When I return, the barrister has all but finished with me. But the worst is to come. I know because I've been warned about

Jono's barrister by my brief. Apparently, he's ruthless and hates women. Great.

'Ms Roseland, he begins. You say that my client raped you and set fire to your house. Are you some kind of fantasist?'

I don't look at him and remain silent.

'Ms Roseland?'

I glance at the jury and fiddle with my rings.

'Ms Roseland?'

The judge removes his spectacles and addresses the barrister. 'I believe we have ascertained that the witness is known as *Mrs* Roseland. Would you do her the courtesy of addressing her correctly?'

One nil to me! I allow a slight smirk to cross my face. *You'll need to try harder than that to intimidate me, matey.*

'My apologies Your Honour. Mrs Roseland.' He stabs me with impossibly blue eyes. I repeat, you say that my client raped you and set fire to your house. Is that correct?'

'It is.' I feel tall and strong. *Bring it on.*

'And you saw him light the fire, did you? Saw him strike the match?'

'No.'

'I see. And you say he raped you. Isn't it true you had always made your body freely available to Mr. Symonds? 'Promiscuous' was how he described you.'

I'm thinking hard. This answer needs to be right.

'I had finished the relationship several weeks before he raped me. Sexual consent is not a given right. A man should know that when a relationship is over, the sexual component ends with it.' *Not bad.*

'So, we only have your word for it that Mr Symonds raped you. You neither reported it to the police nor attended hospital. Is that correct?'

'It is.' I look at the jury and hope they can see that I'm truthful.

'And the reason this 'alleged rape' was kept secret?'

'Embarrassment. I felt stupid that I'd allowed him into my house.'

'I see. Do you often make irresponsible decisions Mrs Roseland?

'Like everyone. Sometimes I do.'

'I believe it is a matter of record that you have had affairs with married men before Mr Symonds. Is that correct?'

'Yes.'

'So having an affair with Mr Symonds was just part of your lifestyle. Is it fair to say that you are not, how shall I put it…. over-bothered about the status of men you sleep with?'

'No. We won't say that. This time it was very different. I was single and had an affair with a man who I believed was free.

'I see. But was it not you who enticed Mr Symonds into your bed – were you not lonely? After the death of your husband.'

What a heartless thing to bring up. 'No. I repeat, I was free to start a new relationship and Jono hid the fact that he was married. Jono Symonds lied to me and concealed his marital status for months.'

On day three his wife is called to give evidence. She looks rather sweet in a childish kind of way; small, even petit, with expensively highlighted hair. Those padded shoulders dwarf her but are very 'of the moment.' A nod to Lady Di. Her silk dress is a pale grey with a white lace collar, and she exudes an aura of shy schoolgirl which makes her look vulnerable. *She's definitely dressed to raise sympathy.*

She is part of the defence team, of course, but the prosecution wants a go at her too, and she looks as petrified as I was. A small bead of sweat sits on her top lip and she falters over the oath. Under different circumstances we might have been friends. The prosecuting barrister begins his examination.

'Could you tell the court about your husband's state of mind around the autumn of last year? Shall we say between September and Christmas?'

I notice her swallow and then stretch her left hand as if trying on a glove. A look of concentration washed her pretty face and then she's ready.

'Are you referring to his medication?'

'I'm asking in general terms Mrs Symonds. How were things within the home? Within the marriage? Was Mr Symonds behaving in a normal way?'

'There is no 'normal' behaviour for Jono.'

'Could you explain what you mean? Give us some details perhaps?'

She faces the public gallery, scans their faces, clearly looking for moral support. *Poor cow. And it's my fault. If I hadn't had an affair with her husband, he'd never have set fire to my house. I wonder if she's got a poppy waving in the breeze to support her, too?*

She looks ready for the stressful task. 'As you know Jono has a complex mental illness which can be controlled by medication. He's had it since he was a teenager and it's well-documented.

'Please continue Mrs Symonds.'

'He...He doesn't always take his pills. Or sometimes he only takes some of them. He says he gets fed up with the side effects.'

'And what signals to you that he isn't taking them? Does he tell you?'

'No. I can tell by his... behaviour. He becomes agitated; he gets a kind of personality high. He becomes hard to live with because he thinks he can manipulate the whole world. And he frightens the children....and me, sometimes.' It's a mousy squeak and her eyes hit the ground.

She's afraid of him.

I catch her glance across the court to the dock, but Jono shows no flicker of recognition. *I wonder if that hurt.* She's broken his trust by speaking out and he won't forgive her. He'll punish her if they don't lock him up. Just like he punished me. But I can look at him now. He's not a threat because I've given my evidence and he's harmless. He's also statuesque, stunningly handsome with not a hair out of place. Today he's in a pale grey suit with a jaunty tie and…I still love him. Oh no you don't.

'And was he displaying signs that he was off his medication, would you say?'

'No, he was not.'

'Not off his medication?

'No. He was taking them until after Christmas.'

'Please tell the court how you justify that statement Mrs Symonds. Was it more than a 'gut feeling' that Mr Symonds was taking his medication??'

'One of my duties as his wife is to make sure he gets repeat prescriptions on time. That he never runs out of pills. So, I always know when he stops taking them.'

Duties as a wife?' OMG she sounds like a Stepford wife.

'I see. So just to be clear about this, are you telling the court that your husband was taking his medication between September and Christmas last year?'

'Yes.' She takes a lady-like sip of water.

'I'm sorry to be blunt Mrs Symonds but did you know your husband was having an affair during this time?'

'Of course. Not only do I know when he has an affair, but he always tells me who the woman of the moment is.'

Oh God. He actually told her about me.

'Forgive me, but you make it sound as if your husband is a serial adulterer.

'He is. He takes his pills when he's hunting for fun... and comes off them when it's over. That's why it's so easy for him to pick up women. He's a very plausible man when he's stable. Charming and a good liar.'

Hell's teeth. She's lived with his philandering for years. She's immune to it.

I suddenly long to have Chris sitting beside me, to feel the warmth of my husband's hand and to know everything will be alright. *But it won't be alright, will it? It'll be all over the newspapers and I'll be a scarlet woman.* I start to have thoughts about the children being teased at school. Bullied and taunted about their mother. *Maybe I should move away and make a new start.*

'So, are you swearing under oath, Mrs Symonds that when your husband allegedly set fire to Mrs Roseland's house on November 19th last year, he was taking his medication?'

'Yes. To the best of my knowledge, he was.

'No more questions your Honour.'

It took four days for most of the evidence to be given. Day five was the worst for me as Jono took the stand. He wore a pale blue shirt that day with a fine white stripe. His navy blue tie offset his dark blue suit. He looked every inch the fuckable rogue.

He told them I loved him and begged him to leave his family. He said I had been in relationships with married men before and that he was just another notch on my belt. He said he never loved me, and I became a nuisance to him.

I can forgive his lies; after all, he's under immense pressure and knows he's going to prison. But to say he never loved me...that really hurts.

Two medical men give evidence that Jono has a complex personality disorder, and a symptom of that illness is his belief he can turn any situation to his advantage. Someone called him manipulative. And dangerous. *What have I done to my children? Will they ever forgive or forget the fire? Probably not. Why can't I be a normal mother? It's not as if I don't love them to bits. I love them more than life itself, but I keep screwing up.*

The outcome was Jono got fifteen years for arson and attempted murder which seems lenient from where I'm standing, but probably feels like a life sentence to him.

Chapter 20

The decision to tell Veronica and George about Jono was taken out of Kate's hands. It would have been hard to hide a smoking, burnt out building and a well-documented court case. But her new-found family were supportive. There had been no scolding, just sympathy and cake.

George was able to suggest reliable workmen, and he was happy to oversee any issues around the rebuilding of the garage and kitchen. The relationship between the families grew closer by the month. Often Veronica made a delicious meal for Kate to pop in the oven and as they all sat down to a family supper, there were many 'pinch me' moments. The children loved it.

Kate had known changes were essential and she'd made a pledge to create a healthier lifestyle and take a more pragmatic attitude towards men. She'd been physically drained by the trauma and heartache caused by Jono Symonds. Somewhere amongst the turmoil, she knew she had to take responsibility for her own bad decisions. She also had to face the village after so much of her personal life had been spread across the local rag. She needed to hold her head high and move forward.

Soon after the court case Susie's 'cut through the dross of life' attitude had helped Kate realise two major choices needed her consideration. She could find a new job and stay with all the familiar networks she valued, including her birth mother who was beginning to be important to her, or move away from the area and hide from all the publicity and heartache. The latter would have created more issues than it solved and on reflection felt foolhardy. She'd never been a head in the sand kind of woman. Also, within the melting pot of decisions, was her dread of 'leaving Chris in the house.' Everything they'd built together was written in the brick walls. Eventually, moving away was eliminated.

Kate had two priorities - the children and the repairs to their home. But busy as this kept her, nothing could keep her mind off Jono Symonds. She couldn't defend the strong feelings she still held and dared not tell Susie. She'd even caught herself worrying about how Jono was coping in prison.

No one could accuse her of lethargy. She joined a singing group in the village and helped with a coffee morning for the children's school. But he haunted her, part lost lover and part liar, cheat, and arsonist.

Sleepless nights and daily self-doubt impacted on Kate's good intention to change. She gave notice to her employer at the nursing home, partly because she imagined Jono lurking around every corner. She could see him in her office and still sense his beautiful body and feel his touch. Her head space was on over-load.

Eventually the house was repaired, and she was able to re-create the home they had treasured before the fire. Kate never wanted to see building dust or hear loud radios ever again. But she was grateful that the insurance had paid for the work, allowing life to get back on an even keel.

Kate pondered her future, safe in the knowledge that she had no money worries in the short term. She could afford the luxury of thinking everything through before making decisions. Good decisions. They had to be good decisions, this time.

She decided to find a yoga class and before long became adept at downward dog. She also joined a group who walked and talked while taking much needed fresh air. At first it sounded lame but soon proved her wrong. She began to look forward to the fortnightly gatherings.

After several months Kate regained a degree of equilibrium and was ready to find a new job. Life at home had become boring with her children at school all day. So, on a whim she applied for a Medical Representative post with a major pharmaceutical company in the area which included her home county of Gloucestershire. When she was offered the job, she embraced the new challenge of introducing her company's medicines to GP's and hospital doctors with a planned outcome that they would prescribe them for their patients. She could only hope she'd made the right decision.

'Of course, it's perfect for you Katie. And we can all ensure there is no back-sliding over that slug. God only knows how he got so far under your skin.'

It was easy.

There was a flurry of excitement as she prepared for her new working life. A new wardrobe was a must and she and Susie spent hours getting everything just right.

'Stylish but definitely not tarty,' announced Susie.

'Just what are you saying? Kate asked in mock dismay.

'You know exactly what I mean. No leopard skin sundress for a start.'

'I love that dress. Who's to say a GP wouldn't find it riveting?'

Susie shoved Kate's arm. 'You know perfectly well what I mean. At least, I hope you do. I wonder if the medical profession in Gloucestershire is ready for Kate Roseland. Somebody had better warn them.'

Two days before Kate was due on the training course in Basingstoke, her brand spanking new Daytona yellow Ford arrived. A knock on the door revealed a uniformed delivery guy who, in return for her signature, had handed Kate the keys to her company car. The children had been beside themselves with excitement.

'Cool colour Mum,' Tom announced as he jumped inside.

'Pink would have been cooler, but it'll do.' The closest thing to praise from Hannah.

Poppy and Susie helped with the children while Kate was away for a four week training course. Luckily, she'd been able to get home at weekends.

'How's the talent? Susie wanted to know.

'Just because I'm the only woman on the course doesn't mean I intend to work my way around the male fraternity.'

'I'm pleased to hear it.'

'I didn't say one or two aren't interesting, in their own way.'

'Hmm.

The training was no push-over and even with her nursing knowledge, she'd needed to work hard to pass out at the end. She'd insisted on standing her round at the bar in the evenings and made sure she did plenty of studying at night. Kate spent half an hour on the phone with the kids each evening and heard about their day at school. And there'd been nothing to indicate they were missing her. They were turning out to be independent kids.

When the training course ended, Kate took up her new post, supported for the first couple of weeks by her area manager. She found her work schedule very different from her nursing home job but before she'd embarked on her new career, she'd managed to find a local girl who was looking for a job with children and wanted to train to be a Nanny. It was agreed that Laura would take the teatime shift with the children and stay with them until Kate got home, and if things worked out well, it could lead to longer hours.

Some days Kate managed to take the children to school. If she had an early start, which was always the case when her area manager was with her, then Susie was willing to help. The school holidays were some way off, but Kate hoped Laura would step up and make a proper job of it. She could even live in if she wanted to.

Life was uncomplicated for a while.

Kate was having coffee with Susie one Saturday when she imparted to her friend a small detail which was bothering her. 'A guy who was on the training course wants to meet up for a drink. He'll have to drive about ninety miles to do it. What do you think?'

'For God's sake Katie, can't you give men a rest for a while?' What do you think he wants if he's prepared to make nearly a two hundred mile round trip?' True to form Susie said it as she saw it. 'Greg and I want to put you on a leash. You need containing.'

'Umm...I've often wonder what the call for leather whips and black boots might be around here. You kinky thing Susie!'

'You know what I mean.' Susie chuckled at her incorrigible friend.

Kate, however, decided there was some truth in Susie's sentiment. So, to preserve herself for the foreseeable future she decided that rather than give up men altogether, she'd treat them like items on a restaurant menu. She would pick and choose those she liked and diet on a regular basis to recharge the batteries. There was a massive healing process to get through but if the odd dalliance helped, who was she to argue?

Kate's resolve held for a while. Batting away male interest held its own amusement value and, before long, she'd become proficient. Although she had the occasional blip.

Unfortunately for her many pledges to stay celibate, there was something about young skin that intoxicated her. A certain fragrance, or was it the softness or the perfection? All were attributes that were wasted on the young, who took everything for granted.

Kate had been unable to reject this one, such was his appeal. Her silky skinned hunk writhed under her touch and hardened as she stroked his penis with experienced finger. He moaned in orgasm. She stroked his legs and caressed his perfect, long back; she nibbled his ear and licked his cheek before nudging the tip of her tongue between his cupid-bow lips. He'd opened every inch of his body to her caress, and she'd teased and denied him relief until he'd begged for it.

Now, he was sleeping like a child. Long languid and young, he'd surely need sex again when he woke. Speckled sunshine lit his torso and rested golden highlights on his hair. His body-warmth smelled of chocolate. Half man, half boy. Delicious. His desire for her was insatiable and the catnap would soon have him hard and eager again.

She'd picked up this glorious creature while making a visit to the county hospital. He was playing at being a porter to get money before university, while she was every inch the power dressed businesswoman looking for the orthopaedic consultant. He knew where she'd find him but suggested he took her through the various lift systems.

'It's complicated in here. People get lost every day,' he told her.

'Heaven forbid we get lost,' Kate quipped with a smile as she took in his delicious body. A bit David Essex she thought. He must be all of eighteen. That was fair game in her book.

Kate studied him further.

'Do you always look at people like that?' he ventured, his cheeks a Japanese sun.

'Only when they're as good looking as you,' she replied, fixing him with a twinkle in her eyes.

He blushed some more, and the loud ding reminded them they'd reached level three.

'If you turn left and take the third door on the right, you'll find Mr. Wang's secretary. I'm sure she'll be able to help.'

'You've been a great help. Sorry, I didn't catch your name.

'Ben. I'm Ben, and yours is?'

'Friends call me Kate.'

'Could I be a friend and buy you coffee when you've finished with your appointment?'

Hmm... he's not shy then.

Ben and Kate became fucking buddies for about three months. They sensibly laid down ground rules. No emotional attachment, always use a condom, and when he went up to Durham to start his degree, it would be a clean break.

The new job suited Kate. It offered flexibility, challenge and was mostly male oriented. What was not to like? Every day brought different tasks and best of all, the children hardly noticed the variation in her routine. Laura accepted Kate's offer of more hours and the children liked her, so the childcare pressure was lifted and Kate didn't need to stress about asking too much of friends.

One busy Monday morning, after a little frustration and the odd swear word, Kate had managed to park her car in a hospital carpark. *Why don't they make spaces bigger?* She was almost late for an appointment and grabbed her briefcase and walked as quickly as her three inch heels would allow. A glance at her watch told her she had four minutes to get to the other side of the building and find the Special Clinic, which was euphemistically known to all and sundry as the Clap Joint. She could just make it.

She'd met Dr Pete Lewis once before and he'd shown some interest in her medical products, and possibly her body. Kate was quick to spot a *'come on'* but Pete had a naturally relaxed and friendly personality, and she was cautious about making a snap decision. She was in no hurry, although Ben had been in Durham for a couple of months, and she was ready for pastures new.

The nurse had showed her into a small, green-painted, cheerless room where she'd mingled with waiting patients. It felt uncomfortable. Her mind became fixated on suppurating genitals.

'I'm afraid Dr Lewis is running late. I've told him you're here and he asked if you'd wait.'

'I'll wait.' Kate had a flexible morning and a half hour or so was neither here nor there. But the notices on the walls freaked her out. 'Tell your sexual partners you have an STD.' *Imagine having to do that.*

'Have you any of the following symptoms?' This was one step too far. Kate wondered what attracted a doctor to Special Clinic. Especially one as good-looking as Pete Lewis. She'd browsed the grubby selection of magazines and checked her watch a couple of time. Eventually she'd heard a chair scrape in the consulting room and a white coat appeared with an attractive man inside it.

'Hi. Kate? My colleague will finish the list.' He'd held out his hand.

'Yes. Dr Lewis. We met about two months ago at Julian Booth's retirement lunch.'

'Oh, I remember it well. Come.' He'd led her down a corridor and into a side room. 'Sorry the facilities are far from salubrious, but at least they're private.'

'I'm pleased about that. I was beginning to get funny looks in the waiting room.'

'You get used to funny looks in my line of work. But ladies find me fascinating at drinks parties, although I've no idea why.'

I have.

Kate had taken the only other chair available as they sat to discuss her products. 'You said you have used cephalexin when you were on ortho. Have you tried it here?

'It's not my first-line drug Kate.'

'I know you have a raft of penicillens to call on, but this is a real alternative if you have allergic reaction to consider. Available as oral, intramuscular, and of course intravenous, although you won't have call for that here, I guess.'

'I suppose price has always been a factor. Penicillens are so cheap.'

'Cephalexin can't compete on price, you're right, and as you know we also make penicillin. But I'm hoping to convince you that it's a good alternative; a second option for patients who aren't run-of-mill; maybe patients who return often and become immune to first-line drugs.'

'Mmm. We do get a few of those. I'll think about it. Do you have some samples?'

'Sure. Kate had bent to take them from her briefcase. 'When you need to consider a patient's alcoholic consumption, that's another good option. Although absorption is slightly impaired, there is no contra-indication with alcohol or recreational drugs using cephalosporins.

'You've got a bit of competition in this hospital Kate. I believe pharmacy is buying basic penicillin from Glaxo.

'That's a dirty word Dr Lewis! Sounds like I need to meet this pharmacist who clearly needs persuading away from the competition.'

'I should think you have a fighting chance at that. Tell Henry I sent you.'

'I will.'

'To be fair, I'm happy to give it a go. Perhaps for UTI's to begin with. Is it safe in pregnancy?'

'Yes. You can prescribe with confidence to pregnant women.'

Pete Lewis looked at his watch. 'Have you got time for a cup of tea? The staff dining room isn't anything special, but they do nice biscuits.'

'Done. I'm a sucker for a good biscuit.'

They'd taken the maze of corridors and lifts and arrived in a smallish restaurant with cheery red Formica tables and grey chairs.

'Grab a seat and I'll organise it.'

Kate had looked at him and noticed his attractive brown eyes and a slightly cock-eyed eyebrow that had a mind of its own. She'd chosen a window as far from others as possible and Pete was back almost as soon as she sat down.

'Our tea will be delivered,' he announced, 'by the wonderful Florence who makes the biscuits.'

'Impressive,' said Kate. 'Especially for hospital catering.'

'She's a gem and unfortunately due to retire at the end of the year. Life just won't be the same without her.'

Kate had studied the handsome face and wondered what the body was like.

'So, how do you like the job? I remember you're a nurse.'

He remembered our conversation at Julian Booth's retirement do. Hmm...

'It's certainly different. But I enjoy the travelling and most doctors are a bit of a challenge.'

He shot her a look. 'Guess I'd better not fall too quickly for the glib product knowledge then, or anything else. I don't want you to think I'm a push-over.'

'How about I label you a breath of fresh air? Would that do?'

Florence arrived with a pot of tea for two and a biscuit arrangement fit for the Ritz.

'How lovely,' said Kate.' I hear your biscuits come highly recommended.'

'Don't go believing anything he tells you. He's a proper flatterer, he is.'

'How can you call me a flatterer Florence? Just look at Kate here. Does she think I'm flattering her? No. She sees a serious doctor with nothing in mind but his patients.'

I really think he's giving me a come on.

'I'm not susceptible to flattery Florence. Only to doctors who prescribe my products,' Kate chipped in.

'Well, you can't be too careful with this one,' she'd said as she walked away chuckling at her own joke.

'Seems your reputation goes before you.'

'Don't believe everything you hear about me Kate. Don't suppose there's any chance of a little bit of a lunchtime do is there? We special clinic bods get over-looked by drug companies all the time.'

'Is that how to get you prescribing doctor?' Kate gave him a cheeky smile and rummaged for her diary.

'As if a few bottles of wine would ever influence my better judgement.'

'In my limited experience it loosens the pen, at least for a few weeks. And that gives the product a fighting chance.

'Too wise, too soon. You've been talking to other company reps.'

'You're right. I have. What day is best for lunch? Any good on a Friday?

'Fridays are OK, but Wednesday is better.'

'How about four weeks today?'

Pete gave her a grin. 'That would be great. Where are you thinking?'

'How many in the department?'

'How does just one sound?'

Kate could feel the colour rise in her cheeks. *For God's sake, you're not a child. Go for it.*

'I can handle one,' she quipped. 'Where would you suggest?'

'As a married man I think out of town would be good.'

Well, no lies here than.

'Do you know the Ploughshare on the Chippenham Road? It's a good lunch stop, and the service is quick.'

'Not too keen on quick service.' Kate smiled and wrote the date in her diary. 'I have a healthy budget as I've not been in the job long. Do you have a good appetite?'

'Voracious.'

Kate took another biscuit, more for something to do than from hunger.

'That's a date then,' Pete told her. I'll want to sample all the goodies... pens are always useful, and that Glaxo rep has small head torches. Brilliant they are.'

'You're wicked. I'll do my best.' Kate gathered her briefcase and her modesty and thanked him for his hospitality.

'You ain't seen nothing yet,' he'd told her in Broadway slang. He'd grinned and lifted one eyebrow.

I'm sure it was the left one last time.

The pending lunch date caused Kate more than a little consternation. Should she dress to impress, or should she throw on whatever came to hand, arrive late and be every inch the overworked rep? Hmm...who was kidding who here? The final decision was a new scarlet skirt she'd bought for work but which hadn't yet had an outing, her white voile blouse that gave a hint of snowy-white underwear and small heels as she remembered he wasn't as tall as she usually liked her men. The sun looked ready to stay all day and she only had one practice of five doctors to see in the morning. Perfect.

Pete arrived first and Kate had watched from the far end of the carpark where she'd lingered behind a copy of The Times. His Triumph Stag suggested he was a playful kind of guy. Just her type. Kate couldn't resist peeping at her latest conquest. He was wearing casual slacks, and a navy blazer and she'd noted his firm chin and confident walk. She gave him a minute before she moved the car closer to the pub and casually made an entrance.

He'd spotted her immediately from the bar where he was ordering a gin and tonic. He touched her shoulder.

'What can I get you Kate?'

'The same for me. Bombay please.'

'A lady after my own heart. Our table is over in the corner. Do go over and I'll bring the drinks.'

She'd eaten little. Talked even less but used the art of being a good listener to perfection. Pete had talked about anything and everything as they enjoyed the house-special of cottage pie and fresh vegetables.

'This place doesn't give even a nod to fine dining, but the grub is always tasty. Is yours OK?'

'It's delicious. But I have to say, anything I haven't cooked always tastes good and any improvement on the kid's fish fingers gets my vote.'

'Then I shall have to treat you to lunch more often.'

'I think you'll find I'm treating you on my expenses today. Wasn't that the deal?'

'Oh yes. Sassy and loaded. Do they come any better?'

Kate smiled and ordered trifle from the menu. 'It's old fashioned but I really fancy it today.'

'Probably not as much as I fancy you.'

It didn't sound corny; it made Kate melt when she saw the desire in his eyes.

They ended up in bed as Kate knew they would. It was a pub with rooms, very convenient and Kate suspected he was an adulterer who knew his way around. These days Kate's lingerie was in two distinct categories; she liked Marks and Spencer for everyday and Cavendish House for such occasions as today. But she'd made a point of never hanging any underwear on the line since the horrendous experience with Jono.

Pete Lewis had all the charm of a perfect lover. He'd arranged champagne in the room which was cold and delicious; his mouth was gentle, and his hands knew how to please her. And all this before he satisfied his own need. He'd kept their conversation on topics to amuse her and very far away from his home and family. She knew the score.

'Shall we empty the bottle?' he'd asked. It would be a shame to waste good champagne.'

'Mmm…Do you have any time constraints?'

'I'm curious. Do you?'

'No, actually ……

He'd removed her glass and kissed her deeply. 'I love champagne kisses, don't you?'

'That's verging on corny,' she'd laughed. 'Stop talking while I show my appreciation.' Kate kissed him from his head to his toes and sensed him hardening beneath her. She licked his stomach and giggled when he begged, 'lower, lower.'

Chapter 21

Kate

I'd been curious about Gran for many months. She of my foster home fame. For me she was still the lady who held the secret to my early life and also the giver of a quarter of my family genes. After I had found Veronica, I fully expected her to take me to see my grandmother. But it hadn't happened, and as time went on, I'd found it too tricky to broach the subject, for whatever reason.

I'd become curious to discover if she was the lady I remembered. That period of my childhood, more than any other, was rife with abandonment and she'd done her best to make up for the hand life had dealt a small girl.

I'd wondered how the 'big girls' had turned out. Those raucous, lipstick-smeared girls who gave me anguish and too little bed space, must now have families of their own. And they were my aunts. I'd played with the words, but they'd made no sense and I wondered how they felt about my return to the fold. Nothing guaranteed acceptance and I was aware that I was setting myself up for further rejection. I could have stood next to them in the supermarket and not known them. And what about the long-suffering son, Ed, who'd lived in a hormone-fuelled house? How did he ever get near a mirror to shave with all those sisters clambering for attention? And did he remember the little scrap who watched him wash under the outside tap?

I could wait no longer.

No one knew about my plans except Susie. I'd bought a small bunch of flowers, nothing ostentatious, and driven to the village with a degree of excitement. It's not every day a girl gets the chance to catch up on grandparents she hasn't seen for twenty five years.

I'd made my way up the stone pathway and knocked on the door. My heart was beating like a kettle drum. I could hear a shuffling inside and knew someone was in although it was an age before the door was opened. A marshmallow lady stood before me with a familiar wrinkled face and hands that had grafted all their lives. I'd searched for a smile but there was no hint of welcome, no warmth in her eyes. She'd looked no older than the last time I'd seen her.

'I heard you was back.'

Not exactly what I'd hoped for. 'I...I'm Kate.'

'I can see who you are.'

'I wanted to call and say hello. Is it a good time? Are you busy?' I felt ridiculously nervous. *Buck up.*

'Always busy, me.'

'Umm...would another day...be more convenient? I could call again if you'd rather.'

'No. Best have a look at you. See how you turned out.' She'd turned her back on me and marched down the hallway. I wasn't sure if I was meant to follow so I stood still and waited to be invited.

'You coming or not?' *She's not big on manners.*

'Yes. Of course.' I looked at my shoes which were wet from the cloudburst that had hit the village as I parked my car. 'I'll slip my shoes off. Shall I?'

'No need for fancy ways in this house. Just shut the door, the cold's crippling me.'

I found myself in the sitting room where I'd drunk sherry with my mother and George. Now I noticed the signs that it was an old lady's domain with antimacassars, china ducks and tasselled cushions. I had not spotted them before. China ladies in dance dresses, cats and pixies, and there was a mustiness in the air I hadn't sensed before, either. I thought the flowers a mistake but gave them to her anyway.

'Never did like pinks. Stink they do.'

At least I was brought up to have manners. And that's the first Brownie point I've ever given Bitch-Mother.

'Veronica and George were doing your garden when I called last time. It was a bit of a shock…to come face to face with my mother. I think you were shopping in Gloucester.' I noticed the sherry decanter on the sideboard had been refilled.

'Twood 'ave been best if you'd never come.' *Even more to the point than Susie.* She sat in an armchair which she filled to perfection. Her ample body settled like scum on a boiled ham. She poked the small coal fire and didn't utter another word. I began to feel she'd said all she intended to when she turned and stared at me. Was she seeking reassurance I was part of her clan, I wondered, or did she see her own daughter in me?

'You goin' to stand there all day? Sit your backside down.'

I'd done as commanded. I remember I'd pulled my dress down over my knees like a kid. I counted pixies on the shelf.

I've never been good with silence. I'm the one who always jumps in with an inane comment if there's an awkward lull in conversations. But I'd held back that day. After all, she'd invited me in. This was her call. Eventually, just as I thought I'd leave, she'd turned to look at me.

'Y'er like yer mother.'

'I suppose I am.' I look at the photo above the fire. 'George called us peas in a pod.' I was beginning to wonder if my visit was a mistake.

'The past is best left where 'tis. Did no one ever tell you that?'

She thinks I have no right to be here. 'I'm happy to go. I don't want to upset you.'

'Sit yerself down and stop blathering.'

Now I'm stuffed. I can't leave without appearing rude and it looks as if she's going to give me a piece of her mind. Funny, I remember her as a lovely lady...Hell... I'm not putting up with this.

I stand up and move towards the door. 'I'm sorry to inconvenience you Gr...Mrs Oswald. There's no reason why you should want to meet me. I see that now. I remember you as a kind lady...'

'Sit yer bum down and don't go all la de da on me.'

I did as I was told.

'If yer mother 'adn't been 'ere when you called, I'd never 'ad told you where she lived. Isn't right. Let bygones be bygones, I say.' She poked the fire until it looked as if it might expire.

'Shall I tell you what I say, Mrs Oswald? I say that kids who are pushed around and don't know their parents, deserve better treatment than you're giving me. Now, before I say something I shouldn't, I think I'll go.' I marched out of the door and headlong into an elderly man with a white beard and a thatch of white hair.

'Whoa there. You nearly knocked me over. What's the hurry?'

'I'm sorry. I'm leaving before I get very cross with the women in there. She's supposed to be my grandmother though you'd never think it. And tell her she'll put the bloody fire out if she pokes it anymore,' I added and felt hugely better for saying it.

'Well, I'll be blowed! Is it little Katie? Got your mother's hair. And your Aunt Cath's temper, I shouldn't wonder.''

'Are you Mr. Oswald?' *Of course he is Dummy. Don't suppose she's got a live-in lover these days.* I was so cross I could hardly look at him.

'I am indeed although I think that's Gramps to you.'

'I shouldn't let your wife hear you say that. She wishes I'd stayed away.'

'Ssh, her bark's worse than her bite. Come on in and I'll sort her out.'

He took my arm and led me back into the sitting room. 'Annie. Put the kettle on. We've got a visitor.'

Gran did indeed have a fierce bark and I could testify to that. I got the feeling few people stood up to her. And she didn't put the kettle on, but she was less acerbic in her husband's presence.

'Haven't you not made the girl a cup of tea?'

'She's not stopping. Got a lot of la de da ways as far as I can see.'

'Now I've found Veronica, I......well, I hoped you might be pleased to see me, too.'

'Course we are. Come and park your backside next to Gran. Looks like I'll be making the tea.'

'Please don't bother on my behalf. I've got to collect my children from school soon.'

'We heard you've got a couple of kiddies. Didn't we Mother?'

'Everybody's got kids in our family. I 'spose a couple more can't do no harm.'

'I only came to say hello. And there are a couple of things that have been...well, bugging me, I suppose.'

'Ere we go. Spit it out then.' Gran looked as if she could kill me.

You don't have to sit here. Just go.

Gramp gave his wife a sharp look. 'Ask away. Not sure if we'll remember, but you can try.'

OK, this is your chance. Get it off your chest. You've waited long enough.

'What I want to know is why no one told me who my mother was when I lived with you?' I threw the comment into the air. Either of them could answer. I wasn't fussed.

'Wasn't done in those days. Still a bit of a... stigma, if, you know what I mean.' It was Gramp who proffered an answer, poor as it was.

'I know exactly what you mean. I've lived with it all my life.'

'Don't suppose you had many problems once you got with those la de da new parents of yours. I 'eard you was spoilt.' Gran was still poking the life out of the fire.

'Well, it may surprise you to know that sometimes you're wrong in your opinions. Things aren't always what they seem. But I haven't come here to talk about them.'

'She gets on her high horse just like our Christine, don't she?'

'Pipe down Annie. The girl means no harm.'

'Best if she'd stayed away.'

I was angry now and sorry I'd called. She was obviously a prejudiced old biddy, and I was wasting my time. 'I remember you as kind. You used to be lovely to me.'

'Memory can play tricks.' She studied her nails and nothing more was forthcoming.

'Nice little maid you were.' Gramps studied me with tired eyes. 'Couldn't keep you at our house for long, you see, but you were a right little ray of sunshine.'

'Miserable little cow you was. You spent all the daylight hours on that wall. Do you remember that wall?'

This was flagging up red signals. I was that little girl again with scuffed sandals and a yearning for Daddy Fred to bring the doll in the box. *Don't let her bring you down Kate. Stand up to her.*

'Yes, I remember that wall and the misery that engulfed a small child who...deserved better. *This is no time for a blub Kate.* I was just a little girl who didn't ask for all the crap life had thrown her way but....do you know what? I survived, and my children have never felt unloved or unwanted. Think on that Mrs. Oswald.' With that I stomped out and by the time I reached my car I was shaking so much I struggled to get the key in the door.

I'd sat in stunned silence, amazed that an old woman, my own grandmother, could be so insensitive and vitriolic. Quite why I was surprised, after living with Bitch-Mother, I'd no idea.

I'd gone home and cried my eyes out. *What a wimp. You're like dopey Dorothy; you're always chasing rainbows and happy endings. There is no yellow brick road for you Kate Roseland, just hard tarmac and you might as well start walking it. Got it?* I'd got it.

Chapter 22

Kate slipped into a relationship with Veronica and George that was comfortable. It wasn't exactly like silk stockings on a dancer's legs, but she felt able to pop in if she was in the area or ring to suggest meeting up for lunch. The children had taken the new additions to their family in their stride. What was so interesting about two more boring adults in their young lives? Kate hadn't been over-explicit with them, but they'd taken her scant explanation on board and asked no questions. They'd already known Mummy had a weird childhood and they liked George and Veronica who could be relied on to provide sweets and toys.

But was her row with Gran about to change things? Kate had taken time to absorb the horrors of her visit to her grandparents and knew Veronica would already have the details, no doubt delivered quicker than a carrier pigeon. Kate pondered over what had gone wrong. Could she have gone about it differently? Perhaps she should have asked Veronica's advice, she could have discussed her desire to see Gran instead of charging in with her usual enthusiasm.

Kate had an appointment to see a GP practice where the doctors were prescribing one of her products and she needed to check if they were happy with the results. As it was only three miles from Veronica and George's home, she'd decided to call in for coffee. She knew George would be busy with his hospital car run, but Veronica was always pleased to see her. She liked to hear about Kate's job and what the children had been up to. Kate needed to be watchful that she and George didn't spoil Hannah and Tom as they tended to buy expensive presents when there was no occasion to celebrate.

'Just look on it as me giving them all the things I never gave you,' Veronica had told Kate by way of explanation. Her eyes had a habit of filling with tears whenever the lost years were mentioned.

'That's fine, up to a point,' Kate told her. 'But it worries me when I hear Hannah asking for a new bike. She's already a handful to deal with and she's not reached her teens yet. I don't want her to look on you as a money tree.'

'I know. You are right and George tries to curb my spending. They are both so lovely. It's hard, but I'll try.'

Veronica was delighted when Kate called for coffee. She'd appeared her usual self but there was little chance that she didn't know about the disastrous visit to Gran. She'd brought a Victoria sandwich from the kitchen.

'I must have known you were coming,' she said as the aroma of baking made Kate's mouth water.

Kate thought she looked pensive. As if something was on her mind.

'I've just made it,' she announced as she cut a generous portion for Kate. 'It's still slightly warm. George so loves a bit of cake.'

'Not good for the waistline, but delicious,' said Kate, licking icing sugar from her fingers. 'Shall I fetch the coffee? '

'Could you dear? Thank you.' Veronica fussed with coasters and plates before she sat down next to the rubber plant. 'I think that's George's car.' She'd bobbed up to the window and waved. 'He can smell cake a mile away.'

She's twitchy today. Something's brewing and it's not the coffee.

'I thought he was on hospital cars today,' Kate said as she brought two mugs of coffee and placed them on the side table.'

'Usually he is, but he's swapped his shift. He's just been to get a few bits from the shop. He probably looked in on Mum and Dad, too.'

'Oh. I hope he gets a better reception than I did.' *Straight for the jugular, that's the way.*

'I'm so sorry Kate. Mum told me you called. I gather she was a bit blunt. It's just her way. That generation don't believe in *'airing dirty washing in public,'* as Mum would say. I got quite a roasting when I told her about you. That you'd called here when she was out.'

'I've been called worse than dirty washing.'

'Oh no. The dirty washing is all mine, I can assure you. Please don't misunderstand Kate.'

'I appear to have been nothing but trouble since I found you.'

George came in bringing a gust of fresh air in his wake. 'Who's been trouble? Not me I hope.'

'Hello George. No. It's me that seems to have caused trouble.'

'Oh. You mean your visit to see Mum and Dad? Brave girl; straight into the lion's den. We should have told you how she felt about...all this.'

'No. It's my fault. I should have told you I wanted to see them instead of barging in, uninvited.'

'No real harm done. You look as if you can stand up for yourself. You're not an Oswald if you can't. Working in the village today, are you? Giving old Dr Crouch a grilling?

'Something like that.'

'I'm just in time for coffee, I see.'

'I'll do it dear.'

'No. I can make a cup of coffee. You talk to Kate.'

He'd returned with a steaming mug and sat next to his wife on the leather sofa.

'Nice bit of cake.'

'I suggest you wipe the icing sugar off your nose dear. It's not a good look.'

And then there had been an uncomfortable silence.

'Is something wrong? You seem not your usual self today, Veronica.'

Kate caught a look she threw at George before busying herself with her cup of coffee. 'Anyone for a top-up?'

I'm not good with charged atmospheres. 'Do say it if something needs saying. I'm a tough cookie you know.'

'There is something we wanted to talk to you about, dear. The next time you popped in without the children.' George looked at his wife.

'Fire away. I'm practically flame-proof.'

'Kate, we worry about you.'

'That's a first for me. Having someone worry about me is a whole new experience.'

'Oh dear. I...George, tell Kate what we heard.'

'I think you should tell her. It's your friend who said it.'

'Now I'm beginning to feel worried. Gossip and rumour tend to follow me.'

'Well...sometimes it feels that... let's say you don't always appear to make choices that are kind to yourself.' Veronica fiddled with a button on her dress.

'What kind of choices? What do you mean exactly by *'kind'*?'

'Um...well, men really. I mean the men you seem to be mixed up with.'

'You mean I screw around? Is that another way of saying it?' Kate could feel her colour rising.

'I don't think Veronica would put it like that Kate. It's just that, well we worry about you.' George chewed a bit of skin around his thumb. 'A friend of ours saw you with a doctor from Swindon Hospital who happens to live next door to her son and his family. Pat and Ron, remember? They met you when we had Sunday lunch in the Plough. Well, we aren't sure if you know this doctor has a family.'

Kate could feel a full blown blush creeping up her neck.

'Men can be frugal with the truth if they fancy an attractive woman.' Veronica avoided eye contact with Kate.

'As I said, we worry about you, that's all,' George garbled. Then he'd closed his mouth and looked at his wife.

'Well please don't worry. I'm a grownup you know. Even if you blinked and missed it.' *Careful. That was a little near the mark.*

'Let's not fall out Kate. Veronica has waited so long to know you and I think emotions are running high.'

'It's taken me over two years to start living my life again after losing Chris. My friends are…they're pleased I've started dating again.'

'Yes, yes, I'm sure it's a healthy sign but, what worries us is'…George had looked at his watch for the third time. 'We think … no, actually we know that this doctor is married.' It was Veronica's turn to look uncomfortable.

'A married man? And you want to lecture me because…?'

'Let's not say anything we'll regret dear.' Veronica plumped a cushion that was already plump and stared at her perfect nails. *You can tell she's never brought up kids or done much housework.*

'No. I agree. Why don't we have another bit of cake? Your mother makes a damn good cake, doesn't she?'

'And another thing dear.' *So much for not saying anything she'll regret.* 'I can't help thinking that maybe your adopted mother tried hard but with you...but you were a difficult child. We know someone who saw you grow up and, well it all sounded so brutal the way you told us.'

'A difficult child! How could I not be?' Kate tried to gather her temper but failed. 'I was passed around like a parcel somebody left on a bus. Of course I was a difficult child.'

'I'm so sorry you feel like that about your upbringing Kate. I shall feel guilty for the rest of my life. We only want...what's best for you. But married men will lead to more unhappiness. Don't you think? Trust me, I know.'

'I'll tell you what I think, shall I? It's hard to take lessons on morality from someone who gave away not one baby, but two.' Kate could feel the flush of temper in her cheeks. Not something that happened too often.

The shock on Veronica's face told the whole story. Her second secret had been laid bare, told to Kate by a manipulative, younger sister who had spilled the beans but forgotten to mention it to Veronica. *Families, eh?* So, baby Lionel was my brother. Did no one think to tell me?'

'Let's put the kettle on again, shall we?' George was legging it into the kitchen. 'I'll make us some more coffee.'

'No. I haven't time. I have an appointment.'

'Oh dear. This isn't a good way to leave things. Are you sure you don't have ten minutes dear?'

'No. I've waited a couple of months to see this surgery and I can't be late.' Kate gathered her handbag and pea coat and walked into the hall. The sooner she got out the less she was likely to say. *Bloody hypocritical woman.*

'We'll ring, won't we dear? And we're looking forward to Tom's Halloween show. What did you say he is? A pumpkin?

Kate neither acknowledged the comments nor said goodbye. She was down the stone pathway and into her car before they had time to draw breath. *Bloody cheek. Listening to tittle tattle.*

After Kate had seen the doctors in the local practice, she called on Susie. Was it to dump the fury her mother had instilled in her? Probably.

'Isn't it bad enough to have one Bitch-Mother without having two?'

'Hold your horses, Kate. Hang on a minute. I don't expect Veronica meant any harm. It probably wasn't a critical conversation. I expect she worries about you. We all do.'

'So, it's you as well. You think I'm a slapper, too?'

'No one is calling you a slapper. It's just with all this talk of HIV...it makes sense to be careful.'

'And nurses don't know how to be careful, I suppose?'

'Oh God. Why must you be like this? Can't you see we all care about you?'

'I'm *like this* because I'm flawed goods and screwing men makes me feel good.'

Susie closed the kitchen door. Her youngest was at home with a temperature and she was alarmed he might be listening to the conversation.

'Listen Kate and listen well. You are way off the mark here. Veronica has tried to forge... well it's a delicate relationship, at best, and you're about to chuck it all away. From the little I've seen of her she seems kind and I know she's sorry for giving you away. You're such a plonker sometimes.'

'Thank you. So, I'm a slapper and a plonker? And a liar according to Veronica who thinks I had a perfect childhood and I've made everything up about Bitch-Mother. Do you think this relationship is going anywhere but down the pan?'

'Listen to me Kate. Pin your ears back and listen. It wasn't your fault that you door-knocked your mother with no preparation, and it wasn't your fault your grandmother rejected you, either. But what might be your fault, are the poor choices you make in men. Don't expect your birth mother to be pleased you're going down the same path she took. She's bound to have problems sitting back and watching you do that.' Susie opened the fridge and poured two glasses of white wine. 'Damn, I never drink in the day.' She pushed one over to Kate.

'I'm never going to invest any emotion in another man after what Jono did to me. So where am I meant to get the odd shag from? Tell me that. Married men are safe Susie. They don't tell. Not unless they're nutters like Jono. But surely there won't be another Jono in my life.'

'You need to take stock of what you're doing. That's all I'm saying. We'd love to see you settled with a nice guy, and in time you will be. Meanwhile, leave the married ones alone.'

'Well at least you've made your feelings clear. Very clear.' Kate grabbed her coat and bag and abandoned the glass of wine Susie had placed in front of her. 'See you.'

While Kate had waited for her daughter to finish her ballet class she mulled the events of the morning. *I can't take criticism from Veronica. She has no bloody right to tell me how to live my life. How many men did she screw around with to produce two illegitimate kids?* But it wasn't about that was it? It was about Kate's inability to accept the growing relationship between them. She had little experience of family dynamics and certainly no idea how to handle disapproval from Veronica. She did what she thought was right.

Dear Veronica, it won't take long to say this. Whichever way I try to unravel the critical things you said, I always come back with the same thought - you are a hypocrite. With your part-confessed past and your second murky little secret, how can I take disapproval from you? At least I know what I am and don't try to hide it under a cloak of respectability. You have no right to tell me how to live my life. You gave me away, albeit with regret, but not enough regret to prevent you birthing another little being, one who presumably went the same way as me.

You are dealing with guilt because your decision to give me away didn't have a happy ending. You don't want to believe that my version of life with Bitch-Mother is true, because it makes you face the horror of your actions. Can you imagine how it felt to finally unburden my childhood on someone who should have cared? But you doubt me. You believe I could make up such horrors. Well, take it from one who knows, it was all true. Let people tell you otherwise if it makes you feel better. You must find your own coping mechanism the same way I had to. And yes, I know I'm damaged and I have a flawed personality, but it's not helpful to have you preach morality.

I don't need you in my life, so please stay away from me and my children.

Chapter 23

Dr Pete Lewis had all the makings of a heartbreaker, but luckily Kate wasn't susceptible. At least once a week he seduced Kate in hotel rooms and plied her with champagne and roses. *I'll take this. A good looking guy with money to spend on me and a joy between the sheets is a rarity. What's not to like?*

After Jono, Kate had vowed she'd never allow a man to get under her skin again, and she intended to stay single for the rest of her life. So why not get her kicks with Pete Lewis? She had no interest in his wife and children, they were boxed away with a 'no go' sign on them, and she was no threat to them, anyway. And if you have no expectations from a man then you can't be hurt.

Pete announced he wanted to take Kate to Vienna. He was attending a medical symposium and was sure there would be no risk of being seen together so far from home. Who would they bump into in Austria?

'A Clap Clinic Conference! Riveting. I'm pleased I don't have to attend.'

'You could take a little retail therapy while I'm busy. We could hit the nightlife after dark.'

'Sounds lovely. I've never been to Vienna. Not that I associate Vienna with retail therapy. Or nightlife, come to that. Are you sure?'

'A colleague told me that it's right up there with other European cities. Is it a deal breaker Kate? The shopping.'

'The only deal breaker could be my kids. I need to ask my friend Susie if she'll have them, and I've been a bit of a bitch lately. I'll need to do some serious grovelling.'

'You a bitch? Surely not. I don't know if I'm more excited about the bitch or the groveller.'

'Never push me too far, Dr Lewis. I spit when cornered.'

'I love feisty women Kate. And your red hair leaves me weak-kneed. So, what are the chances of a few days away?'

'Depends entirely on getting the children cared for. I couldn't enjoy time away with you if they're not happy.'

'Of course. I understand that. I don't have to complete the booking for another week, so you have a few days to sort things out.' He'd taken her hand, 'I can't image waking up to find you in my bed. I think about you all the time.' He'd winced. 'Did I just say that?'

'You did, but it was the wine talking. You're perfectly happy with your home life and you know it. I'm no more than the icing on your cake. A delicious cake. Of course.'

'Mmm. Well, I hope Susie comes up trumps. I'm dreaming about it already.'

'I'm thinking about the architecture. And the shopping.'

'Don't I get a look in? I'm thinking about waking up with you in my bed, naked and ready for love.

'Very lyrical. I'll look forward to it. Provided my children are sorted. I have some bridges to mend, but I'll let you know in a couple of days.'

Kate had taken Susie out for lunch, and it wasn't on her expense account.

'I know what an idiot I am. I'm so sorry Suz. I have no idea how you put up with me.'

'Me neither. You're enough to drive a girl to drink sometimes. But at least I can liven up my own dull existence through your exploits.'

'I know you don't mean that. You wouldn't swap Greg for anything.'

'You're right. I wouldn't, but just sometimes I'd like an injection of mystery.'

Kate and Susie never ran out of things to talk about and for both it was a 'warts and all' friendship. Susie said she would be delighted to have the children for three days. 'It's about time you started having fun.' She didn't ask who was taking Kate to Vienna. 'You're tired from coping and it'll do you good. Good looking, is he? This mystery man. He must have a healthy credit card.'

'Healthy enough for me. And yes, he's good looking ...and...'

'Stop.' Susie put her fingers in her ears. 'Too much information.'

They laughed and Kate promised to let Susie have the travel arrangements as soon as she could. She felt guilty that she'd not told Susie that it was the delectable, married Pete Lewis, but no one told their friends everything. Did they?

Vienna was cold. A bitter wind blew through Karlsplatz Square and had Kate scurrying into shops. And Pete had been right. Top-end fashion was everywhere. And chocolates. Within the first hour she'd found silk lingerie, an angora sweater and a pair of killer heels that complimented her winter coat. She bought wooden puppets for the children from a street vendor who'd been entrancing a group of children with his amazing prodigies. She knew the girl in pink lace would excite Hannah and the lad with a sausage dog on a lead would amuse Tom. She found a beautiful carved angel for Susie nestling in a window display of Christmas items. It would make a great tree decoration in a couple of months' time.

Kate wanted to find something special for Poppy who had no family of her own, and seldom received gifts. She was a lady of simple tastes, and many of the exotic trinkets displayed would not have been to her liking.

Kate stopped for coffee to refuel her energy levels and then ambled down a side street where she found the perfect gift for her neighbour. A breathtaking display of enamelled poppies shone in an artisan jeweller's shop and she watched as the handsome young assistant wrapped her chosen poppy in tissue paper. He placed it inside a small box before creating a cacophony of ribbons on the lid. He handed it to Kate with a killer smile.

'Madam. I 'ope you enjoy it.'

'Thank you. I will.'

Kate had been due to meet Pete at five o'clock in the hotel bar and she could already taste her first gin and tonic. It had surprised her how exhausted she'd felt after shopping most of the afternoon. They'd had a leisurely breakfast together in their room and Pete had displayed the Do Not Disturb sign on the door as he left.

'Make sure you're up before I get back. No. On the other hand, be sure you're in bed when I return.'

'You're a randy old goat, do you know that? I shall absorb the atmosphere, the culture and the architecture of Vienna. Then I shall shop 'til I drop. I may be tired when you get back,' she teased.

'I'll soon change that,' Pete laughed. He handed her a wad of foreign currency. 'Enjoy your day. See you later.'

They had tickets for Vivaldi's Four Seasons that evening which was to be performed in a small church close to the hotel. She'd been looking forward to spending time with Pete without having sex as the major event on the agenda. They had lots in common and an easy relationship had developed, but the nature of the beast kept them in clandestine venues and always on time limits which weren't conducive to small talk. But not so this weekend.

Kate arrived first in the bar, ordered her G&T and charged it to the room. She perched on a bar stool and knew her endless legs looked good under a short black dress with a jewelled collar. Very Audrey Hepburn she'd thought when she bought it in Cheltenham, especially for the trip to Vienna. She wondered how her knees would cope with the chilly wind when they went outside later, but a girl needs to suffer for fashion, doesn't she? She wished she had a long coat; she'd seen a stunning fur specimen earlier which was rather Dr Zhivago, but it had a price tag which had made her eyes water, and she would never wear animal fur.

Pete arrived late. After a quick kiss he went to their room to shower and change. Kate was on her second gin when he reappeared.

'I'm so sorry.' He ordered a drink. 'You look ravishing. Are you sure you want dinner and Vivaldi? I can think of something even more exciting.'

'You're lucky I'm still waiting. I nearly took up a better offer.'

'I promise I'll be worth the wait.' He kissed her lightly. 'Tell me about the retail therapy.'

'Much more interesting than a clap lecture, I'll bet.'

'How can it be more interesting than pustules and rashes?'

'Oh Lord. Is that how you spent your day?'

'Shall we eat? I've booked an early table, so we'll be in time for the concert.'

'Sounds good to me.'

They did their best to eat frugally from an astounding array of rich food on the menu. Kate ordered hake on the bone while Pete made a grand gesture of demolishing a venison steak without sauce. They were only just in time for the concert and had to persuade the door keeper that they would be as quiet as the grave if he let them creep in. The crescendo of music was heavenly. Pete had stroked her hand and smiled. He too was enjoying their unfettered time together. After a quick, chilly walk back to their hotel the remainder of the night was spent in pure carnal pleasure.

Kate enjoyed her few days in Vienna but was ready to come home to her children on their last day. Her old friend 'guilt' tried to creep in. Guilt about Pete's family. But she willed herself to ignore a small inner voice, no more than a tiny buzz in her brain, asking if she was getting tired of her promiscuous life? Maybe.

Chapter 24

Kate

Bitch-Mother is dead. Alleluia. How do I know? My adoptive father knocked on my door two days ago to give me the news. He is a shadow of a man, worn down I imagine by a lifetime of hell with Bitch-Mother.

He was timid as indeed he should have been. He couldn't quite meet my eyes. He stood on my doorstep looking as if the world had worn him to a frazzle, as if something had taken big chunks from him.

I was flooded with memories. I was a small child again, desperate to be loved. A little girl left to the mercy of a woman who should never have been within fifty miles of a child, especially a fragile one. She, who had no idea what a human child needed, and he, who watched on like a hopeless prawn. They were adults and should have known better.

I invited him in. It felt the polite thing to do. 'How did you find me.' I asked.

'Your mother and I have known where you live since about a month after you arrived in the village Katherine. Word spreads like wildfire. You must know that.'

'So, you know all about me losing Chris.'

'We did. It must have been a struggle. I'm so sorry for your loss.'

'Sorry. Is that all you are sorry for?' My tears fall as if a dam has burst.

'No Katherine. It's not all.' His head slumps like a weary work horse. 'I know I am a weak man. And now I have a terminal illness. I'll shortly follow your mother into the grave. I had to come and see you.'

I want to tell him to piss off, but no words come from my lips and the tears continue to flow.

'I know I can never make amends, much as I would like to. It was her you see. She had a vendetta against you and when....'

'The court case. You can say it.'

'Well, yes, the court case and the terrible fire. She said it proved she'd been right all along. It was hard to argue with her as I expect you remember.'

'No. But I remember the beatings and the nosebleeds and the gun. Oh, you probably never heard about the gun. Not the truth, anyway.' I'm hot and damp with tears and losing control of pent up emotions I've carried for twenty five years. 'I tried to shoot myself when I was ten. With your shotgun. What do you think of that?'

If he'd looked old and frail when he'd arrived, he looked shrivelled and broken after I'd told him some home truths. And then I felt sorry for him.

I made us a cup of tea and found biscuits I'd made for the children. He was like a mirage. Sitting on *my* sofa, in *my* house. I could see life had rinsed him to nothing.

'I'm so sorry Katherine. I wasn't the father you deserved. You were such a sweet child. Always anxious to please.'

'But there was no pleasing *her*. Was there?'

'Neither for you nor for me Katherine.'

He was still struggling to make eye contact but I grasped the nettle to slay the elephant in the room.

'Listen Dad. My childhood was a disaster from the day I was born. Your wife added layers of damage, some of which I carry today. But it's over. I don't harbour grudges, especially not to you.' I was unable to stem the tears, but I was crying for that little girl, not the person I am today.

'I don't deserve such generosity, Katherine. Thank you.' He munched on a biscuit and stared at a photo of Chris and the children. 'What are your children's names? I've seen them a couple of times. One day when they took their bikes on the common, I was walking mother's dogs, and suddenly there you all were.'

I thought about his words and curbed my need to remonstrate his weakness. Could he not have spoken to us? But would I have wanted him to? We'll never know and somehow, I don't care. 'I'm Kate, Dad. Call me Kate. And my children are Hannah and Tom.' Perhaps I could have been a little kinder.

'I want to ask you something, Kate. Would you read a poem at your mother's funeral?'

A red mist descends. I go to the kitchen to fetch a box of tissues and to calm myself. When I return, I'm strident and strong. 'Will *no* suffice?' I look at him in amazement that he would ask me to attend her funeral.

'I understand.'

'And don't add my name to any family flowers, either.'

A silence gathers as we drink our tea.

'There was something else I thought I should tell you.' He looks at me. 'I've left the house to you. It seems the least I can do.'

'What makes you think I would want the house where I tried to kill myself because of the miserable life you and that woman inflicted on me?'

'Oh Kate. Such hurt and hatred. I feel responsible.'

'Oh, you are. Believe me, you are.' And then I feel less angry, less sad, and less of a victim. Now she's gone. And having said words to my father that were long overdue, it's allowing me to lay my childhood to rest. 'But it's in the past, Dad. I've moved on and I guess you will to.' *Whoops. He told me he's dying. Crass.*

'But not for long.' He digs in his jacket and brings out an envelope. 'My will. This is a copy of my will.'

I don't take it and he lays it on the coffee table.

'I can't accept it. I could never live with myself if I accepted money from that house. However, if you redo your will and leave it to the children, I won't object.'

'I'll do that Kate. I don't suppose...you would let me meet them? No. No of course you wouldn't. Why would you?'

I feel the bigger person. The adult to his child. 'Yes. We can arrange that. Perhaps you would like to come to lunch on Sunday.'

He died two months later, and I read a poem at his funeral. True to his word he left the house and a chunk of money to Hannah and Tom.

Chapter 25

Kate

Another Christmas Eve and we're all a year older. Hannah has adopted a religious attitude to Christmas this year, due in part to her friendship with the daughter of the local vicar.

'Christingle is at five o'clock Mummy. And you mustn't have a drink before you enter God's House.'

'Must I not? I'll be sober as a judge, I promise.'

'You do know the Lord's Prayer, don't you?'

'I think I can just about manage it word perfect. Is it important at Christingle?'

'Of course, it is. Everyone should know the Lord's prayer.' She gives a concerned expression so like her father that my heart skips. It's hard to keep a straight face, but her earnest sentiment about Christmas this year is touching, and she hates to be laughed at.

I have issues of my own to confront over the next few hours. I'm cooking Christmas lunch for Susie and the family as a thank you for their unstinting support. Poppy is also invited. I can't imagine how I would have got through the last three years without my stalwarts. It feels like big-time pay-back and I'm up for it.

But it's not only the cooking I have on my mind. The turkey is in the shed, placed up high away from the mice, and the booze cupboard is stocked to capacity. I've already packed the children's stockings, although there are one or two last minute things still to do.

Why do we always reminisce at Christmas? I suppose it's a nostalgic time for most people. This will be Christmas number two without Chris, and it feels a little easier for all of us. Undoubtedly, my life is more settled, and the children are growing like weeds, seemingly unscathed by the death of their father. Chris is a natural component of our family conversations, and we regularly share our memories and the fact that he is still missed. And we still 'jiggle' the fairy lights on the tree.

I love my job. I've now devised a routine and know most of my GP's. The affair with Pete Lewis ran its course with no broken hearts or regrets. And he still prescribes my products. Win win! But tomorrow feels like a huge milestone and I'm nervous; I feel sixteen again.

I've invited Jake to Christmas lunch, and he'll bring his four year old, motherless daughter, Lily. I've met her a few times and she's a darling, but it will be a big day for her tomorrow. I have yet to work out the logistics of seating ten for lunch, and that's before I consider seating strangers among people who know each other well. It's bound to be hectic. I don't want Lily or Jake to feel overwhelmed, but Jake said he'll take her home mid-afternoon if things get too tricky.

I've told Susie and Poppy about my tentative, new relationship and they couldn't be more pleased, but I've yet to break the news to the children.

 'Have you checked his marital status and his health record?' Only Susie could come up with that.

'Yes, on both counts. His wife Becky died of cancer eighteen months ago and, although I wouldn't be surprised if he's still a bit wobbly, he's amazingly strong. And he's a brilliant father.'

'Well so far, so good.'

'Damned with faint praise, I think they call that.'

Susie laughed. 'You know there's nothing in the world I'd rather witness right now than you and the kids happy again. Whether the 'bug-man' is the right one, who knows? I'll reserve judgement until after lunch tomorrow.'

'Don't call him that. It'll stick. He's Jake Hayward, consultant microbiologist, to you.'

'Hmm...but what is he to you?'

On Christmas morning I was awake early, even earlier than the kids. As the dawn broke, I noticed a strange light creeping through the curtains, it was yellow and unusual. I lay in bed a few minutes longer but couldn't contain my curiosity. As I threw back the curtains I shrieked with delight. Snow. There was about an inch on the roof of the house opposite and a sugar coating on the larch wood fence. The gravel was nowhere to be seen.

I jumped out of my warm bed and grabbed my dressing gown. 'Tom, Tom. Hannah. Wake up.' What parent in their right mind wakes their children on Christmas morning?

Two sleepy children stirred as I threw open their curtains. 'How many times have you wished for snow on Christmas Day Tom? Look. Look it's a winter wonderland in our back garden.'

And then the excitement began. I put the turkey in the oven, pleased that I'd remembered, then we dressed in our warmest clothes and rubber boots and stormed outside to play. I had to put on both the kitchen light and the outside light to illuminate the garden.

'Can we build a snowman Mum?'

'We can do anything we want. It's…Christmas!'

After half an hour a sombre snowman was presiding over the garden, resplendent in an old coat of Chris's that had remained on a peg in the utility room. Mr. White, as he was christened, borrowed Hannah's school scarf and we were one carrot short for lunch. Snow Angels glistened at his feet. My two delighted children began to shiver.

'Who's for hot chocolate?'

'Me. Me.'

We stamped the snow from our feet and shed clothes to dry in the utility room. Soon we were perched on barstools in the kitchen where the big bird, stuffed the night before, was already wafting delicious aromas our way.

'Let's open stockings,' I suggested.

'Yeh!' Hannah and Tom rampaged up the stairs and came back with excited faces, grasping their Christmas stockings.

We all sat on the sheepskin rug in the sitting room where I soon had the log fire roaring. I put Carols from Eton College on the tape deck.

'We have two extra guests for lunch,' I ventured.

'More than two,' said Hannah.

'I mean two extra, extra guests. We'll be ten around the table this year.'

I could see Hannah doing the mental arithmetic. 'OK spill the beans.'

Was she eight or eighteen?

'We've invited a friend and his little girl. Jake is someone I met at work. His little girl Lily lost her Mummy almost two years ago and I don't want them to be on their own today.'

'Hasn't he got a boy too?'

'Sorry. Just one girl.'

Tom was disappointed.

'How old is she?' Hannah looked ready to strop.

'She's only four Darling. She'll need a big girl to help her through the day, I expect.'

'Oh...she's little. I can help her unwrap presents. Has she got any presents in our house?'

'She certainly has. And tomorrow we are going to visit Veronica and George. It's been a while, hasn't it?'

'Yeah!' A harmony of agreement from the children would help Boxing Day become a day for reconciliation.

After the scurry to open their stockings, I enticed them both to eat a breakfast of maple syrup on pancakes.

They say Christmas is a time for forgiving and luckily for me we have an invitation to spend Boxing Day with my birth mother and George. And we've accepted. I hope we can put things back on an even keel. I think I've grown up in the last year and I've shed the trauma of my childhood for good. What trauma?

Could this be the best Christmas since Chris died? I do believe it could.

Printed in Great Britain
by Amazon

45996573R00129